Finger Bones

Sara Stinson

DEDICATION

For everyone who helped and believed in me.

Table of Contents

Chapter One   An Old Friend   9

Chapter Two   The Choosing   21

Chapter Three   Secrets   32

Chapter Four   The Angry Ghost   37

Chapter Five   Time Will Come   48

Chapter Six   The Fire   57

Chapter Seven   The Trunk   67

Chapter Eight   The Scarab Beetle   77

Chapter Nine   Grapples   92

Chapter Ten   Mirror in the Room   100

Chapter Eleven Through Thick and Thin 109

Chapter Twelve Graveyard Dirt 121

Chapter Thirteen The Journal 133

Chapter Fourteen Newspaper Articles 145

Chapter Fifteen The Poem 165

Chapter Sixteen Train Trestle 176

Chapter Seventeen Meeting on the Playground 189

Chapter Eighteen Book Report 207

Chapter Nineteen Ghost From the River 211

Chapter Twenty Ghost Hunting 223

Chapter Twenty-one Old Jail House 230

Chapter Twenty-two Kidnapped 244

Chapter Twenty-three The Gift 259

Chapter Twenty-four Obsidian Stones 267

Chapter Twenty five The Witch 278

Chapter Twenty-six The Cemetery 290

Chapter Twenty-seven The Full Moon 301

Chapter Twenty-eight Bubblegum and TV Guides 308

Chapter Twenty-nine Good Enough For Me 324

ACKNOWLEDGEMENTS

First, thanks to Bradley Wind, the Illustrator for the book. Special thanks to Christa Jean Hobart for her Illustration of the moon.

Thanks to Donnie for his patience. Thanks also to my children Kendall and Donnie Jr. for their encouragement. Special thanks also to all Coffee County teachers, staff, and students. They were my pep squad. Finally and especially, thanks to all who read the manuscript and offered helpful and critical insights.

Chapter One

The locals called him Finger Bones.

His name was Charles P. Moody, and for 122 years, he had lived on a dirt road in an old, ramshackle cabin. The road was called Screaming Hollow Road, and it ran alongside part of Bone River which curled around the small town of Bridgeville.

No one ever went up Screaming Hollow Road at night, especially alone. Strange things happened up there, and quite frankly, it was a scary place. And as for Finger Bones' cabin, no one dared to step near the front porch. Mr. Dugmore, a night watchman for the town, witnessed strange lights and eerie moaning noises coming from the cabin. Mr. Murkett, a railroad conductor, told of odd fogs that lingered and cold spots on the land that could chill the bones. Mrs. Lottie swore when she was a young girl she saw ghosts that floated in and out of the windows. And Mr. Fickleburg, the oldest gentleman in

Bridgeville, besides Finger Bones himself, blamed Finger Bones for all the happenings.

Finger Bones lived alone in his house. Every morning he walked to town wearing the same tattered clothes, overalls, and a black hat. His brown eyes looked gentle and his brown face, a grandpa face. The hair on top of his head spread downward into a full beard the color of every gray imaginable. Propped over his shoulder was a stick held by his dark, bony fingers. To the end of the stick a red, burlap sack was tied. No one ever saw him without it.

The street lights gave a dull yellow glow on the pavement as he ambled down Ann Street. Stores were lined together on his right. He casually passed the high school and then the elementary school on his left. Reaching the end of Ann Street, he crossed West Street and went straight to his favorite bench, which was located between the police station and the library.

From early dawn till dusk, he sat and watched nothing in particular. A few of the merchants and locals would pass

Finger Bones avoiding his gaze. Some were afraid terrible things might happen if they ventured too close. When passing by, they would cross the street and turn their heads away from him.

But there were two sweet ladies, Mrs. Mimi Elsie Taylor and Mrs. Caroline Jean Harper, who treated Finger Bones with kindness and didn't consider him odd. Mrs. Taylor was the town's librarian and had been for as long as anyone could remember. Her sister, Mrs. Harper, owned the local jewelry store called, *The Bridgeville Jewel Box*. Both were considered upstanding citizens of the community. They had lived in Bridgeville all their lives. They had never met a stranger, or forgotten a name. Of course, a few of the locals felt the sisters, mingling with this strange old man, were as odd as Finger Bones himself. But the sisters didn't seem to mind what they thought.

Most of Finger Bones' family and friends had passed away between forty-five to fifty years before. Mrs. Taylor and Mrs. Harper were his family now. Although the community couldn't understand why, the sisters doted on him. Mrs. Taylor

could simply bake the best rum cake in Bridgeville. And Mrs.
Harper grilled the best barbequed chicken. At least once a
week, one of the ladies could be found sitting at the bench with
Finger Bones. Each sat laughing, talking, and munching with
an oversized napkin stuffed in their shirts.

It's fair to say many of the children in Bridgeville were
scared of Finger Bones. They were raised to believe he was a
child snatcher. For generations, parents in this small town had
told rumors of how the old man took children who didn't obey
their parents and stuffed them in his burlap sack. He then
carried the children back to his cabin and kept them in a secret
dungeon underneath his bed. However, there was one young
girl who thought different from most kids.

***

Wendy Dee Winkelmann was her name. She was ten
years old. She had known Finger Bones for a year and two
months and now considered him a good friend. Wendy met
him one afternoon sitting at his favorite bench. Along with the
sisters, her parents liked Finger Bones. They told her he had a

heart of gold, and not to be influenced by the gossip. They approved of her spending time with him. Wendy knew the horrid stories, but she also knew the rumors simply were not true and wouldn't tolerate such nonsense prattled in front of her.

On Tuesday and Thursday afternoons, Wendy did volunteer work at the Bridgeville Public Library. She had worked there for as long as she had known Finger Bones. The pain and stiffness from arthritis hurt Mrs. Taylor's hands, especially when holding heavy books. So Wendy was a big help placing books on the shelves, plus she liked helping Mrs. Taylor, and Mrs. Taylor seemed to adore her.

Mrs. Taylor was the reason she loved books and enjoyed reading. The sweet old lady had a way of telling just enough of a story to get her hooked. When Wendy finished her jobs, she would take the book and find a cozy spot in the library, or skip outside to the wooden bench.

She sat with Finger Bones as she read, and sometimes she would even read out loud to him. Wendy never saw him with a book, so she assumed he couldn't read and he seemed to enjoy listening to the stories. She liked hearing his voice, which was deep and soothing. She spent many days on the bench reading and talking to her old friend. Finger Bones told old stories too. Wendy listened with increasing enthusiasm. But little did Wendy know then that the next visit with Finger Bones would be their last together on the old bench.

On that particular Thursday afternoon, Mrs. Taylor recommended a book called *The Shadows* by Jacqueline West. After Mrs. Taylor spun her magic, capturing Wendy's interest in the plot, Wendy chose to go outside and read. She hurried out the doors to show Finger Bones the book.

Immediately she noticed her old friend wasn't sitting at the bench. She came to an abrupt halt. *How strange! He hardly ever leaves the bench during the day for anything.* Wendy gazed all around, but she saw no one. Something in her stomach made a tiny flip-flop. *I'm sure he'll be back in a minute. He's probably gone for a short walk to stretch his legs.*

14

Sitting on her side of the bench, she began reading. She looked up every few seconds looking for her friend, but soon became captivated by the story. Suddenly, she heard someone sit beside her. Wendy lowered her book, turned her head to the right, and smiled with relief. It was Finger Bones.

Wendy wasted no time and started babbling. "Where have you been? I was getting worried, plus, I have the coolest book to read to you today." She glanced over at him as she jabbered, but stopped when she noticed how quiet he was. "Finger Bones, have you been listening to a word I've said?"

Finger Bones sat gazing straight ahead with his hands resting in his lap. He blinked, lightly shook his head, and then looked at Wendy with a small smile. "Oh, yes, I'm listening and would love to hear about the book. Now tell me more."

A glint of something, something dark and red caught Wendy's eyes. She looked down and noticed a trickle of fresh blood, running down the back of Finger Bones' left hand.

"You're bleeding!" she said, jumping from her seat, her eyes wide with fear. "Stay right here and I'll go get my dad." Wendy knew he could help.

His name was Odus Winkelmann and he was the Captain of the Bridgeville Police Department. He knew all kinds of stuff being the Captain. On one occasion, he helped Mrs. Lottie when her car wouldn't crank. He even saved Lloyd Beck's pet raccoon one time from T.R. Miller's hound dogs.

"No, Wendy. It's only a scratch." Finger Bones pointed down to the bench with the one finger, which dripped with blood. "Please, sit down."

"What? No! Your arm doesn't look so good. If you don't want Dad, then I'll call Mom," she said, seeing more blood dripping onto the bench.

Mrs. Flora Winkelmann stayed at home. Although she didn't work, she was a member of many clubs in Bridgeville. She attended meetings quite frequently, both day and night. Thank goodness, Wendy knew today her mom happened to be at home.

"That's the last thing I need at the moment. Now, sit down," he commanded. "I need to talk to you. It's the most important and cannot wait. The arm can wait." He again focused his attention straight ahead.

Her old friend had never raised his voice to her, so she stood there a little startled.

When he finally spoke, he sounded slightly calmer. "After our talk, then all will be fine. It will all work out. It always does."

"What are you talking about, Finger Bones?" Wendy took a step forward, confused. "I don't understand."

"Please, Wendy, sit down and I will explain," he said, lightly patting the bench.

Wendy noticed the dark, red blood now covered the entire hand. She trusted him, but it didn't mean she liked the idea of sitting back down. He was her friend and he was hurt. The blood oozed from his arm and he needed to go to the hospital. She reluctantly sat back down. "Okay, I'm listening."

He wore a tattered, black suit jacket over his overalls. She watched as he reached inside one of the pockets, pulled out a handkerchief, and then maneuvered the jacket off. He tried to sound lighthearted when he spoke to her, but he didn't do a very good job in her opinion. "Tell you what I'll do. I'll wrap my arm with this handkerchief. If you'll tie the ends together it'll be patched up."

Wendy tied the ends.

"Now, the bleeding will stop and I'll be as good as new."

Goosebumps spread all over her body. Finger Bones acted very strange and something was clearly odd about the look in his eyes, and his voice. She had never seen him act so solemnly. He had always been a happy-go-lucky cheerful person. Nothing troubled him…until this day.

They sat quietly side-by-side on the bench, both in their own thoughts. Each stared straight ahead at the Bridgeville courthouse across the street. At the top of the courthouse, the clock tower ticked. The time was four thirty-three in the afternoon.

A cold breeze swept Wendy's face, causing her to shiver. Then another breeze blew. Eerily, this time it felt as though someone touched the back of her hand. Wendy grabbed her hand when a third breeze swept by blowing leaves between them. She looked at Finger Bones out the corner of her eye. He didn't react to the chill. But she did.

The next breeze made her sit straight up, for this breeze also carried with it a voice of what sounded like a man. Wendy heard him say, "Finger Bones. We have cleared the area. We are armed and ready in case anything goes wrong."

Wendy drew in a short breath.

At that point, Wendy watched Finger Bones twist to his right and pick up his stick, which was propped against the bench. The red, burlap bag swayed in the air as he grasped the stick with both hands. He held it horizontal. As he slowly turned to face her, she noticed his large bony knuckles bulging on top.

Those dark bony knuckles, fingers, and hands were famous in Bridgeville. That was the reason for his name, Finger Bones. His oversized bony hands were misfits for his body and were the first things the folks saw when he walked carrying the stick.

He gazed at the stick. "Can you believe I've carried this stick with the bindle on the end for one hundred years?"

Wendy's eyes grew wide. "No way," she whispered.

"I have. That's a long time." He twisted the stick back and forth. "This stick's made of birch. It's a good solid piece that's strong and sturdy." He gripped the stick tightly and gave it a shake. He then looked at Wendy. "Would you like to hold it? Wendy stared at it. Her tummy made a flop. No one had ever held the stick except him.

Chapter Two

Wendy was baffled by such a question from Finger Bones. He had asked her if she would like to hold the very stick and burlap bag he had toted forever. He looked serious. No one had ever held it except him. And why ask now at such a time?

"I'll explain everything soon enough. Here, take the stick," he said, extending it.

Wendy reached out her hands, but then stopped. She thought about her two best friends. "Finger Bones, I bet Claire and Henry won't believe this when I tell them."

"Oh, I think they'll come around, sooner or later," he said, placing the stick in her hands.

Why she didn't throw the stick back at him, turn, and run she'd never know. But something willed her to stay. So there she sat with the stick clasped tightly in her fingers. Suddenly, the stick began to shake in Wendy's hands. Then purplish blue, glowing balls of light emerged from it. The shooting orbs fired in all directions.

"Well, I'll be," Finger Bones said as his eyebrows went up and his forehead wrinkled. "We knew all the signs were leading to you. We just had to be sure. Now we know. It is you," he said in amazement.

Surprised by what was going on, Wendy spoke, her voice getting louder and louder. "Finger Bones, something is happening! The stick…It's shaking! Um, can you explain to me why this stick's shaking? And what's with all the lights? And what do you mean…*it's me*?"

The stick continued to shake. Dancing balls of light flew wildly through the air. With eyes wide, she looked up at Finger Bones. He seemed to be amazed by what was happening. Wendy looked back at the stick thinking she wasn't exactly overjoyed, herself. But being a thinker she didn't panic. And whether he was bothered or not, she had to ask. "Okay, is this a joke?"

The trembling of the stick slowed. The lights dwindled and finally stopped.

Finger Bones gently placed a hand on her shoulder. "Wendy, this is not a trick. It's the stick talking and it never lies."

"Well if it talks, it's got my attention," Wendy said, clenching the stick.

"Have you ever wondered why I'm still around at my age or why I'm in such good health for 122?" he asked, reaching for the bindle.

"I-I guess I have th-thought about it once or twice," she stammered, handing it back to him. "You know, about your age."

"I remember long ago when I had been given the job," Finger Bones said as he laid the bindle in his lap. "I had been twenty-two years old. Now, the stick has chosen you, Wendy, a ten-year-old girl. It knows you have the courage to handle the job." He patted the stick and then continued to speak. "This stick has helped keep me in shape all these many years to accomplish my duties until my time is complete. Wendy, there's a job to be done in Bridgeville. Soon my time will be over. This special stick knows it's time for someone new to do the work."

"What job and what responsibility are you talking about?" Wendy was already rattled. Now she looked at Finger Bones like he was an alien. "You're sounding mighty weird chattering on and on about a stick. And you're freaking me out. I-I think you may have lost too much of your old blood and it's making your brain act scrambled."

"Oh, I've never felt better. And my mind is as sharp as ever," he said in a matter of fact tone, bouncing the stick in his hands. He leaned in toward her and whispered, "I have something very important to tell you, Wendy. Can you keep a secret?"

"Yes sir, I can," she answered, her shock at what had just happened, slowly turning to curiosity. "Why?"

Finger Bones again sat up. He looked around to make sure no one was watching or listening. He looked at her and whispered, "Because the stick and burlap sack are…magic."

"Really? Is that why it made all that commotion?" she asked, scooting closer to him.

"It is indeed. This stick will do other things as well. In my lifetime I couldn't count the number of magical jobs it has performed," he answered with a tinge of enthusiasm.

"WOW!" Wendy touched the stick with the tips of her fingers.

"You've been chosen to do an extraordinary job, Wendy. An important job right here in Bridgeville. And from this day forth, your life will become very different and sometimes hard."

"What important job do I have?"

"Are you listening? This is the most important part," he said.

"Uh huh, I'm listening," she said, drawing closer to him.

"Wendy, you'll have the job of sending ghosts to their next destination," Finger Bones said in a proud voice.

Wendy leaned back and raised her head. She looked at Finger Bones. "I'm sorry. What did you say?" She tilted her head and shook a finger at him. "I could've sworn you just said, 'ghosts.'"

He sat with his head high, holding the stick. Wendy waited for a response, but he did not say a word. He just looked at her and then back at the stick.

"Talk, Finger Bones, say something. You're kidding, right?" She then shook her head and snapped her finger. "Oh, I get it. Did Claire and Henry help you with this one?" She looked around searching for her friends, but she didn't see them.

Strangely, she saw no one walking the streets. No cars drove by or honked their horns. The trees were still. No wind blew and several leaves were suspended in mid-air. Wendy looked up at the clock on the courthouse tower. That's when her eyes really got big. If she hadn't witnessed it herself, she wouldn't believe what she saw. It was still four thirty-three. She was astounded. Everything around them had stopped and frozen in time.

"As I said, Wendy, there are no tricks today. I speak the truth. When the stick chooses, *time* stops for a few moments. Magic is used to keep the townspeople from witnessing the choosing."

Wendy gazed all around her with her mouth opened wide. She was trying hard to figure it all out. Then she remembered the voice. "Finger Bones, I heard someone earlier, and something touched my hand. I didn't see anyone." She turned her eyes to him. "It sounded like a man. Was it a ghost?" she asked, her eyes going wide.

"Yes, it was," Finger Bones said with a gentle smile. "You heard the ghost of Mr. Sam Ballard. He is our Events Director. He was letting me know all was secure in the area."

"Oh." Wendy was in a stupor.

"Wendy, your job's much more than dealing with ghosts. You will also protect the citizens of Bridgeville. There's an evil lurking out there. And we have been chosen to stop it."

"I d-don't understand," she said after shaking herself out of the daze.

"Many years ago, I sat where you sit now. I didn't understand, either. An old lady carried the stick at the time I had been chosen. I asked her some of the same questions you have asked me. And when I held this stick it lit up like the Fourth of July."

"What did *you* do?"

"Oh my, I threw it and took off running," Finger Bones said with a chuckle.

Wendy smiled. "How old were you again?"

"I was twenty-two years old at the time."

"What happened? I mean, she must have gone after you. You have the stick."

"She did. She returned to the cabin after dark while I was asleep. A noise woke me. I sat up and felt this cold breeze in my room. I heard the noise again. It came from outside. I got up from my bed and quietly walked over to the window. Pushing back the curtain, I saw the old woman standing by the barn. She motioned for me to come out.

I had only been married for three months and I definitely didn't want to wake my wife. I hadn't told her about the incident that afternoon. She would have sent me straight to the town's doctor. So, I crept by the bed, slipped on my overalls, and crept out the front door.

That's when the old woman explained everything to me and answered all my questions. She also handed me the stick, along with this burlap bag on the end. The next day, the old woman was found dead on the side of the road. The local paper said she had died of a stroke."

Wendy sat still, soaking in all she had been told. She looked up at a frozen squirrel perched on a tree branch for a moment and then turned to Finger Bones. "So, now I've got to walk around town with that stick every day?" She waved her hands in front of her. "I'm not toting that stick, Finger Bones. I would be laughed out of fourth grade."

"Well the stick has always been handed to the next person when it chooses. But times have changed. I will see what I can do," he smiled. "Even though the stick has spoken, I can still make use of its power for twelve more hours. For now, we at least wanted to see if the stick chose you, and it did."

Wendy thought, as she often did. "Chasing ghosts huh? And there are good ghosts who stick around down here and help?"

"There sure are."

"Can Claire and Henry help too? They are good at hunting things and they can help me find ghosts."

"Yes, your friends can help. But, don't tell them or anybody for right now. Telling someone before you take over could prove to be dangerous. I'll let you know when it is your time. Until then, I want you to carry on as usual with your daily routine."

"Dangerous?"

"Yes, we risk alerting something dark and evil if this gets out too soon. Wendy, there's something sinister going on in Bridgeville. A malicious spirit's growing and has the potential to cause great harm. We have to handle this transfer carefully. You could already be known to whoever or whatever is behind this evil doing."

"I won't tell anyone," she said, scrunching up her face. "I promise, Finger Bones."

"Good," he said, looking at Wendy with his kind old eyes. "You know something? I can remember having many questions when the old lady met me by the barn in the middle of the night. I know you do as well. And I will teach you as she taught me."

Chapter Three

Wendy sat at her desk at school, gazing at the clock. It had not stopped. She knew because she had watched it all day. Outside, during snack time, she picked up a leaf and dropped it. The leaf floated to the ground. It did not freeze in mid-air. The squirrels scuttled across the playground. Not one stood still.

Claire and Henry asked her several times during the day why she acted so funny and why she kept staring at the clock. For now though, Wendy knew she couldn't tell. She had promised to stay silent until Finger Bones said it was time. She needed to be really careful not to draw attention to herself. Yet after spilling her milk at lunch and almost tripping over the janitor's mop bucket in the hallway, she wasn't doing a very good job. She tried to act normal. But for her, when it came to being hush-hush around her two friends, she found acting normal a hard task.

So when the school bell struck three, Wendy ran out the front doors of the school, relieved. She had made it. She'd kept her promise and so far had kept the secret safe. *It's now the weekend. It'll be much easier through the weekend.*

Wendy skipped over to get her bike.

"Hey Wendy, hold on a minute," Henry hollered, coming out of the school with Claire trailing behind him.

Wendy unlocked the wheels of her bike and jerked back on the handlebars.

"What time do you want us at your house this afternoon?" Henry yelled as he jogged closer.

"Oh no, I forgot all about the sleepover," Wendy mumbled.

Wendy's two best friends in the whole wide world, Claire and Henry, were coming over to her house for a sleepover. All three were planning to break their record by building the biggest fort in her bedroom they had ever built. They had looked forward to it all week.

Claire Grace Clark came to Bridgeville in the second grade. She lived with her grandmother. Wendy thought Claire was the smart one. She was also a worry wart and very tender-hearted. She could, and sometimes would, cry on a whim at the slightest things.

Henry T. Bartlett panicked. When frightened, Henry could run like a scared rabbit scampering from Mr. T.R. Miller's hound dogs. He didn't play football like his brother. He didn't care for the game. But when scared, Wendy knew he could run faster than any player on the football team.

Wendy stood holding her bike as Henry and Claire approached. All three were in the fourth grade at Bridgeville Elementary School and Miss Ingram was their teacher. They had been best friends for three years and three months. Through thick and thin, during good times and bad, they really were best friends to the end.

"Uh, I can't do it this weekend," Wendy said in a panic.

"You're so funny, Wendy," Claire giggled. "Now tell us what time."

"Seriously, I can't." Wendy covered her mouth with her hands and gave a fake cough. "I think I have a fever," she said, placing the palm of her hand on her head.

"What a jokester," Henry laughed. "You haven't been sick in over a year. What about five o'clock? There'll be enough daylight to play outside before building the fort."

"I don't know if I can do this, okay?" Wendy let out an exasperated sigh.

"Fine then, Claire and I will do it ourselves," Henry snapped. "Come on Claire." They both walked away, heading for their rides home.

"No, wait guys." Wendy jogged to catch up with them while dragging her bike along with her. "I'm sorry. I've just had so many things going on the last two days." Wendy took a breath and looked down briefly. When she looked back up she produced a small smile. "Okay, five o'clock it is."

"Great!" Claire said. "I can't wait. My grandmother is letting us borrow two of her huge quilts. I told her they would be perfect."

"My mom let us have her bag of clothes pins," Henry said, scrunching up his eyebrows as he glanced at Wendy.

"And Mom gave me three worn-out bed sheets we can use," Wendy said, trying to ignore Henry. "She said some of the sheets had holes in them, but they would serve our purpose. And we already have plenty of blankets."

"I think the fort's going to be awesome, Wendy. It's going to be the best," Claire said. "Henry has been excited all day. Henry, tell her," she encouraged, nudging him in the rib.

"Okay, I'm excited." He nudged Claire back and started to smile.

"Yay," Wendy said, making a big effort to sound enthused.

Chapter Four

Wendy lived on the north side of Bridgeville. She decided to take the shortest route home by riding down Screaming Hollow Road, the road where eerie noises were heard and ghosts were seen by some of the locals. She had heard many in town also tell of a long-neglected cemetery, where some of the earliest citizens of Bridgeville were buried. One of the strangest graves in the lot was that of an old man named Abner Grapples.

She remembered her father telling her about old man Grapples and how he died during a flood. Bridgeville was surrounded by Bone River and, several times throughout the many years, the town had flooded. On this occasion, Mr. Grapples became trapped in the cave and fell in the water as the river rose. Her dad had said Abner Grapples was washed down the river by the swift currents and no one ever found his body.

Mr. Winkelmann told Wendy the town went ahead and placed a simple headstone beside his wife in the cemetery. The mayor didn't know what else to do. Mr. Grapples had no living kin and Mrs. Lorna Grapples died several years before him. Plus, Mr. Grapples had already paid for the headstone. So an empty grave was placed with his name on the headstone.

As Wendy pedaled on toward Screaming Hollow Road, she remembered Mrs. Harper visiting her sister at the library. Mrs. Harper spoke about the cemetery. She told Wendy of century old trees which draped over it. She described their overgrown branches dipping down toward the ground as though they were watching.

"It almost seems the branches are trying to prevent something from crawling out of the ground," Mrs. Harper said in a low voice. "You know, it's very hard to get into the cemetery now. Thick underbrush surrounds the entire area. I visited the graves not long ago. I discovered sage and catnip growing throughout the brush which made it almost impossible to get into the graveyard."

"I wonder why Mrs. Harper went to such a creepy old cemetery in the first place," Wendy said while pedaling just a bit faster. Besides Mr. and Mrs. Grapples, she didn't know the names of anyone else on the old headstones in the cemetery. Mrs. Taylor's husband, Mr. Percy Edmon Taylor, was buried at the new cemetery on the west side of town.

Wendy stopped when she reached the edge of the dirt road. "Okay, creepy," she said out loud, staring straight ahead. "This dirt road didn't look so scary the other day when I knew Finger Bones was at home. I'll pretend he's at home and I'll be okay."

Wendy's plan worked until she reached Finger Bones' cabin. She slammed the brakes on her bike when she spotted the ghost walking across the yard in front of Finger Bones' log cabin. Wendy Dee Winkelmann had never seen a real ghost, but she had read books about them. And everything she had read told her that this was definitely a ghost. First of all, the ghost was transparent. Wendy could see straight through him to the wood pile stacked against the cabin. Second of all, while the ghost tromped across the dirt yard his feet never touched the ground once. He floated just above the ground on a small patch of dark fog.

Wendy jumped off the seat of her bike, her eyes fixed on the ghostly figure. As one hand held on tight to the handlebar, she shoved the other hand deep into her pocket to grab a piece of bubblegum. She had been without bubblegum for the last couple of days. She didn't have any when Finger Bones revealed his news. But that morning, her mom had saved her. She walked into Wendy's room and handed her a brown paper bag full of bubblegum. Wendy had been overjoyed.

She unwrapped and plopped the gum into her mouth. Wendy was a thinker and when she needed to do some serious thinking or had a tough problem to solve, she liked to chew bubblegum. And at this moment, Wendy decided the floating spirit qualified for some serious thinking.

The ghost wore a wide-striped black and white outfit that looked like pajamas. If Wendy hadn't been so dumbfounded, she would have laughed at him. Under his shirt, she saw his huge arms, swaying in rhythm with his large chest. Never once did he move his head, until he reached the end of the cabin. At that point, the floating ghost abruptly halted, then rotated his body in her direction. He narrowed his thick eyebrows in a fixed, angry position and crossed his muscular arms. His bloodshot eyes did not flinch.

Wendy swallowed hard and nearly choked on her gum. She began to feel woozy. She closed her eyes and took a deep breath. An ominous feeling hung in the air and smells of rotten wood, and wet, sticky mud from the river filled her nostrils.

A cold breeze blew against the nape of her neck. She felt the chill run down her flesh. She looked down. *Something weird is going on here and I'm getting creeped out! I'm seeing a ghost, which I might add is an angry ghost. I thought Finger Bones would let me know when it was time for me to take over the job. I didn't think I would see ghosts until then, and he's got the stick.* She gripped her handlebars even tighter. "Oh wow, I'm feeling light-headed," she said. She cupped a hand over her mouth and nose. "And what's with that awful smell?"

Wendy shivered at the thought of dealing with a mad ghost. Just the pungent smell emanating from him was bad enough to run anybody away. Looking at the ground and her head swirling, she said, "Okay, I've got to get a grip. I can handle this. If Finger Bones can do it, I can. I mean it's just a mean and ornery ghost." She scrunched her nose up and lowered her head. "Oh wow! That smell is so gross!"

After a moment, Wendy slowly raised her head to see if the ghost was still there. He was and he was *smirking* at her! She stopped chewing her bubblegum and gasped. Her green eyes grew wide. "He can see me."

Wendy wanted to scream. Yet when her lungs were prepared to yell out, she remembered something very important and slapped a hand over her mouth. "I've got to stay calm," she mumbled quietly. She had once read how ghosts could feel a person's fear, take that negative emotion and become stronger. So as difficult as it was, she managed to stay quiet. But her stomach was another story as it flipped and flopped on the inside like a fresh-caught catfish.

Wendy didn't know how long they stood staring at each other. If she had to guess she would have to say at least fifty years. Although she didn't want to move for fear the ghost might pounce on her, she surely didn't want to stand there for the rest of the day. After a few more moments, she made a decision. While keeping her eyes on the ghost, she would easily scoot up on her bike and casually pedal down the dirt road without the ghost coming after her.

When Wendy took several steps backwards, there was a triumphant look over the ghost's face. She knew he'd figured out what she was going to do. A smirk widened across his lips...then suddenly vanished. His face twisted into a red rage. His eyes narrowed and his left eye began to twitch. He snarled his big teeth, tilted his large head, and pawed the earth's soil with his left foot, then his right. Wendy envisioned before her a bull ready to charge in the arena.

The ghost pounded forward and headed straight for her. She desperately wanted to hop on her bike and pedal away as fast as her legs would move, but they would not budge. She was scared stiff. Wendy panicked and her stomach began

sinking to her knees.

The black fog swirled and boiled under the ghost. With

each stride, he became bolder. She heard him holler, "It is *time*

for you to give me the *watch*!"

Wendy grabbed the handlebars so tight her knuckles

turned white. She didn't know anything about a watch. But

the ghost didn't look as though he was going to listen. So she

leaned back, bit her lips, and prepared for the ghost to attack.

Suddenly, a loud crack sounded. Wendy jumped. A

huge hole appeared in the body of the ghost. She gawked as

the ghost snarled and roared, and then blew up into a million

tiny pieces. Wendy then spun around to find Finger Bones,

standing not twenty feet away with a colt revolver in his hands.

Smoke twirled out the end of the barrel.

"W-what just happened?" Wendy asked, watching the

last of the fog vanish.

"Bullets filled with sea salt," Finger Bones said,

lowering the gun. "An idea I had after a particular gunfighter ghost challenged me to a duel." Finger Bones tilted the gun and looked down at the barrel. "It's been quite a handy invention. The salt in the bullets only irritate the ghosts though and they only disappear for a short period of time. Wendy, I need you to get on your bike and pedal as fast as you can until you're home."

As she prepared to ride off, she looked back at Finger Bones and yelled, "I'll tell my dad when I get home. He can help. He should be home by now."

"No, Wendy! Remember what I told you," he said sternly.

"But, Finger Bones, he could hurt you." Tears welled up in her eyes.

"No one's going to believe us, Wendy," he said, pulling out more bullets from one of his pockets. "I've been fighting and sending ghosts on to their next destination for years. It's what I do. And I will keep fighting until it's your turn."

Wendy's head throbbed and a sickly feeling crept into her stomach. "I'll stay. I can help," she cried.

"Not yet, Wendy. Your turn is coming."

"I've got to do something," she cried.

"Wendy, go home," he said, taking a couple of steps toward her. His eyes were kind, but there was no smile when he looked at her. "Promise me you'll go straight home and tell no one."

"Okay, I promise," she said, trying to sound convincing.

"It will be as it should be. This will be over soon."

"You be careful around that ghost," Wendy said, wiping a tear with the back of her hand. Even though her hands were trembling, she turned and managed to hop on her bike. She pedaled away as fast as her legs would go. *I'm going to get Dad whether Finger Bones likes it or not.*

As she rode away, Finger Bones reached into his pocket and took out a small, suede pouch. He pulled open the drawstring and with his bony hand, scooped out a handful of powdery glitter and slung it towards Wendy. A milky way of

glitter traveled toward her and showered over her like rain.

A smile spread across Wendy's face. Her worried

expression turned to excitement as she thought about the

sleepover.

Chapter Five

When the doorbell rang, Wendy pranced down the stairs and skidded to the door. "Henry, hey, come in. Are you ready to break our record building the fort tonight?"

"Well, I'm glad you're in a better mood," he said, pulling a duffle bag through the door, and carrying a sack of clothespins.

"What are you talking about, Henry? I've been in a good mood all day," she said, taking the bag of clothespins.

Wendy actually did feel great. She was in the best mood she had been in for a long time and was surprisingly being more cheerful than usual. "Hum, I think I have turned a new leaf. My philosophy is no worries."

"Sounds great to me, but you never did worry. Claire is the one who worries."

Claire staggered up behind Henry panting heavily. She had an overnight bag thrown over one shoulder. "Whew, I'm here. I thought I'd die walking the whole way lugging this thing. I wish Grandmother still drove." She shifted the bag and looked at Wendy. "How are you feeling? Do you still feel like you have a fever?" she asked while stepping inside, closing the door behind her. "And, Henry, why were you talking about me being worried? Do I look worried?"

"I rest my case," Henry said with a nod toward Wendy.

Wendy chuckled, but remained quiet. *Those two are so funny. They're always picking at each other. There's never a dull moment that's for sure. Hum, I wonder why Claire asked me if I had a fever.*

"Henry, answer me. I didn't think I was worrying about anything." she babbled, beginning to sound worried.

Henry cocked his head sideways looking at Claire. But before he could spit out one word to explain, Wendy started.

"Do I feel better? Claire, I haven't been feeling bad," she said bluntly. She then threw up her hands and looked at Henry. "And I haven't been in a bad mood. Geez, where have the two of you been all day? " Wendy asked then turned and started up the steps.

"Girls, one minute they're fine and the next minute they act...weird," Henry said. "I can't figure them out." He started up the stairs, shaking his head.

"Hey, I'm a girl and I'm not acting like that. I'm fine," Claire spat and then started following a few steps behind him.

Henry stopped midway when he heard the comment. He turned and glared at her.

Claire, still climbing, almost rammed into him. She halted and looked up. She held out a hand in front of her. "What? I'm just saying it's not me."

Henry did not respond. He just turned, clumping up the stairs in silence.

"Well, it's not me, right?"

Wendy had to giggle. They all were best friends, but acted like siblings. They would fuss one minute and be fine the next. She twirled on her heels and skipped to her room.

After dinner, Wendy and her two friends scurried outside. They chatted on the old walkie-talkies Mr. Winkelmann had given them. They played outside among the pines and oaks until well after dark.

Then it was time. The three hurried back inside to Wendy's bedroom and made a dash for the pile of quilts, blankets, towels, and sheets on the chair. When complete the three crawled past the hanging towel, which was the door, and they scooted inside to admire their work.

Unexpectedly, Mrs. Winkelmann knocked several times on Wendy's bedroom door. "Hello?"

All three jumped.

Claire placed a hand over her heart. "Does she realize what she could've done?"

"I doubt it," Wendy said, rolling her eyes. "What is it Mom? And don't open the door. It's close to the fort and you may knock it down."

"Okay, I won't. But I have fresh popped popcorn and a container full of warm cookies. I guess I'll just offer them to your father."

"Wait," Henry yelled, scrambling out of the fort. "We wouldn't want Mr. Winkelmann to get a stomach ache eating all that food."

Wendy heard Henry open the bedroom door. She crawled to the entrance and swung the towel back. Instantly, her nostrils filled with sweet chocolate. She looked up and Henry was already stuffing one in his mouth.

"I know these chocolate chip cookies can't be good for him. Didn't Mr. Winkelmann say he needed to lose about seven pounds?" he asked, grasping the bowl of popcorn and container of cookies while trying to keep a straight face – and failing – not to burst out laughing.

"Why, yes he did, Henry," Mrs. Winkelmann said playing along. "Thank you for being so concerned for Mr. Winkelmann's health."

"No problem. It was my pleasure."

Henry dropped to his knees. Wendy grabbed the bowls and trays and crawled back into the fort. All three friends sat facing each other again. Wendy held a flashlight. Claire picked up the popcorn. And the very moment Henry picked up the container of cookies, the clock on top of the courthouse in downtown Bridgeville sounded. It was the loudest bell. It sounded every day at twelve noon and every night at midnight. It was now midnight.

The sound of the bell vibrated through the tent, scaring the three. Wendy scooted her knees up under her chin and wrapped her hands around her legs. She clutched the flashlight close with both hands. Claire shook causing the bowl of popcorn she held to fall to the floor. It looked like it was popping a second time. Henry flipped backwards into a row of clothespins which held the towels, sheets, blankets, and quilts together.

"Dad-blame clock scares me half to death every time," Henry yelled while slinging sheets left and right. "It's so loud it makes my heart drop to my toes. Claire, can you flip the light switch on? I can't see a thing."

53

"I can't see my hands in front of my face either," Claire griped.

"Wendy, where are you?" Henry asked. "Did the batteries in the flashlight go dead?"

It wasn't that Wendy didn't want to answer. She could hear them, but simply couldn't respond. Her body wouldn't move.

Suddenly, a crashing noise reverberated throughout Wendy's bedroom. Then there was a clunk and a short pause.

"Who was that?" Henry asked.

"It was me," Claire groaned.

"Are you okay?"

"I'm okay. My foot went into the popcorn bowl." She crawled up to her knees, raised her arm, and reached for the switch located by the bed on the wall.

"How about you, Wendy, are you okay?" he asked.

Wendy did not answer.

"Shake it off, Wendy. It's just the courthouse clock," Henry said, kicking the rest of the sheets from around his legs.

"Oh yeah, Henry? You're talking brave. You jumped and it scared you so bad you did a backwards somersault."

"So you jumped too. You threw the popcorn and now it's tangled up in all those curls of yours."

While they bickered, Wendy stood silent. She faced the southeast window. The flashlight she held flickered on and off. Suddenly, a cold shiver washed over her and she dropped the flashlight. Something wasn't right. She sensed she needed to remember something. *Time*, she had to remember something about the time.

A faint breeze lightly tousled hair. The temperature outside and inside began to drop swiftly. Wendy felt a strong pull toward the window. As she neared it, her long hair glowed as bolts of lightning lit up the night skies.

The thunder rang through Wendy's ears with such force that it made the room vibrate. The sound then formed and turned into words. "I will get what I want, Wendy. I will return and I will take my place, the place I should have been given before," groused a chilling, old crabby voice. "I will return when the moon is full. "And then, I will return them all. Time will come soon."

Wendy trembled, fear crawled to the bone.

Chapter Six

Claire and Henry looked at each other and then at Wendy. A flash caught their attention outside the other bedroom window. Through the southwest side, they saw dark thunderclouds slowly rolling in as if ready to attack a prey.

They edged toward Wendy. Out the southeast window in the same direction Wendy gazed, they discovered what she was fixated on outside her bedroom window. Boiling black smoke rose high above the tall pine and oak trees in the direction of Screaming Hollow Road. The smoke soon covered the clouds in the skies above with colors of orange, yellow, and red. The colors mingled in the blackness.

Henry's eyes went wide. He figured it out! "Oh no, it's Finger Bones' cabin on Screaming Hollow Road," he whispered.

Tears emerged from Claire's big brown eyes. "How terrible," she whimpered.

Wendy was still frozen, unmoving, and now her eyes had glazed over as though she were in another world.

"Oh Wendy," Claire cried, fanning a hand in front of Wendy's face. "Please wake up. You can do it. You can do anything. You're so smart, and so brave. Remember when you stood up to Buck Fergus last year? I remember. I remember like it was yesterday. He had me cornered in the hall and was telling me I wasn't good enough to be in our fourth grade class, or even in our school. When you saw what was happening, you jumped between him and me with your fists balled up in fighting position. You were ready to knock him into next week if he said one more word. And his two goons never made a step toward you. They were scared of you, Wendy."

Wendy did not move.

Henry started snapping his fingers and popping his hands. "Wendy, snap out of it. Come on. You've got to get it together." He paused and looked down at the floor.

Outside the storm battered down and the rain beat against the rooftop. The wind made branches bend, crack, and fall from trees. The limbs hit the ground with a crash.

"Hey Wendy, I know, we'll go downstairs," Henry said, looking up. "I'm sure your mom can tell us what's going on. Come on," he said, motioning with his whole body in the direction of the door. "Everything will be fine. Finger Bones will be okay. He's been through much worse than this you know. He's a tough old buzzard."

Henry talked calmly. He stayed composed on the outside, but on the inside, it was a completely different story. He had worms squirming all in his stomach and a big lump in his throat.

Unexpectedly, the town's fire alarm sounded. Anyone within the city limits of Bridgeville could hear the droning sound getting louder as it blasted through the air. Claire and Henry jumped, but they continued to stand beside Wendy. Both closed their eyes a moment and listened to the whining of the bell. Seconds later the fire trucks were in motion.

"The fire trucks are leaving the station," Henry said, opening his eyes.

"Henry, I've never seen Wendy like this. What are we going to do?" she asked. "Maybe she's in shock. She could've seen the smoke and knew it was Finger Bones' cabin."

"I don't know what we're going to do and I sure don't know what's wrong with her. Wendy's the thinker. I'm good at running."

And with those words, Claire's expression changed. She wiped the tears from her face. "What a great idea, Henry! Run!"

"What?" Henry now not only looked worried, but he appeared confused.

"I mean run! Run and go get Mrs. Winkelmann. If we can't get Wendy to budge, we can bring Mrs. Winkelmann to Wendy. She's downstairs. I heard her talking on the CB radio a second ago to Mr. Winkelmann. He's at the police station. I heard him saying he was headed out to Finger Bones' place."

Claire looked like she was feeling much better now. She waved her hand at Henry. "Now go!"

Henry started to run. He seemed relieved to be able to move his feet.

Claire placed her hand on Wendy's shoulder. "We're not going anywhere, Wendy. You can count on it. Through thick and thin, we're friends till the end."

Wendy's head became light and her eyes became fuzzy. She began to smell an odd, strong odor that burned her nose. It was appalling. The fuzziness in her eyes changed. It turned into a vision, or was she dreaming?

Wendy saw only darkness. No longer could she see inside the safety of her own house, nor did she notice anything familiar from Hardwood Ridge Drive. She stood in a new and different place, and heard a roaring sound. Taking a closer look, she realized it was the swift currents flowing in Bone River.

Turning in the opposite direction, her big eyes grew wide with fear. In front of her was Finger Bones' cabin, and it was engulfed in flames. She stared in horror at the inferno. Her feet and hands turned clammy. Wendy thought she might pass out she felt so weak. The fire roared loudly like it was alive. One moment it was dancing gracefully and the next the fire swarmed in different directions as though it were trying to attack an enemy…or maybe it was the enemy.

The heat of the fire seemed to grow. Droplets of sweat formed on Wendy's temples and dripped down her cheeks. Her chest felt heavy and her breathing grew more difficult. The air filled with smoke covering the trees and ground. Debris floated through the air. Into the fire Wendy gazed. All of a sudden, she saw something moving and took a step to the side to get a better view. For a moment, she saw nothing but the red-hot blazes, but then her eyes went wide. She couldn't believe what she saw. From the innermost part of the flames, he emerged with his head held high and smiling.

It was none other than, Finger Bones! He walked straight towards Wendy. Surprisingly, he was unscathed. He wore his same old overalls with his black hat, carrying his famous stick with the burlap sack.

He stopped about five feet in front of her. His teeth sparkled as he gave his biggest smile. A white glow circled all around him. The brightest sprinkles of glittery sparkles cascaded everywhere with each and every move he made. He bowed, tipping his hat, it twinkled against the moonlight.

"Finger Bones, is it really you?" she asked in disbelief.

Standing straight up again, he placed the hat on his head. "It is me."

"Are you—a ghost, or—an angel?" Wendy asked. The initial shock was leaving her. Curiosity began to take its place.

Finger Bones gave a chuckle. He swung the stick off his shoulder and propped one end on the ground. "Well let's just say someone has decided my job down here isn't finished, Wendy. Like I said yesterday, you and I have some unfinished business to take care of here in Bridgeville. Yes ma'am, we do."

Wendy clapped her hands together once. "That's it! I remember now. It's *time*. It's my time to…" Wendy stopped talking. She bit her lips together and her eyes filled with tears.

63

"Oh no, the fire Finger Bones, you died in the fire." Grief covered her face.

"Yes I did. But I'm where I'm supposed to be now, Wendy. Dry your tears, child," said Finger Bones tenderly, handing her a handkerchief from his pocket.

The pole and burlap bag shimmered and glinted against the darkness, especially when it moved. Finger Bones dropped it to his feet with showers of glitter flashing once more. He squatted. Wendy squatted in front of him. He untied the twine from the sack and handed it to her to hold.

She began to understand. He was going to show her the contents of the sack. No one besides Finger Bones knew what was inside. Never had he opened it in public before for anyone. Wendy stared down at the sack, untied now but not open.

Finger Bones slowly took hold of the top of the sack, but before opening the contents he looked straight into her green eyes. "Now Wendy, you have a job to do. Tomorrow you will go to the river. At the river you are to retrieve an old trunk I have prepared. I will give you specific directions on recovering the trunk. Until then..."

Finger Bones let go of the bindle and stood up. Wendy pointed toward it. She thought maybe he'd forgotten what he was going to do. She knew that forgetting was something old people did after they started staying at home by themselves. Well she did think about the time she forgot her jacket at school. Then there was the time she left her books at home.

But Finger Bones ignored her gestures. He smiled at her with his kind eyes and said, "You will know by tomorrow what I have said tonight. For now, you must go. And Wendy, do not worry your pretty little head about me child. You'll see me again soon enough." As he said the words he started laughing.

***

The storm passed and only rain droplets pattered against the porch below. Wendy's head rested on Claire's lap while Claire sat cross-legged on the floor. At that moment, Mrs. Winkelmann came bounding into the bedroom. Henry followed close behind her with his straight hair flinging in every direction. Both were gasping from sprinting up the stairs. When they dashed into the room, Mrs. Winkelmann and Henry halted abruptly. For Claire was not crying and Wendy was not in a daze…they were giggling!

Henry looked perplexed. "I think they've lost their noodles," he said, scratching his head. They watched Wendy and Claire shake and giggle.

But only Wendy knew why they really laughed as she opened her hand, holding the piece of twine. She knew Finger Bones was okay and he would return. They had unfinished business to take care of in Bridgeville.

Chapter Seven

When Wendy woke the next morning, Claire's left leg was slung over both of Wendy's legs. Claire made little gurgling and wheezing sounds in her sleep. Not wanting to wake her, Wendy carefully lifted Claire's leg and flipped it back on Claire's side of the bed. Then Wendy sat up to get a good look at the room, and to find Henry. The remains of the fort were scattered across the room. But she didn't see him.

Slinging the sheets off, she twisted to the side of the bed and hopped to the floor. Her foot hit the edge of something. "Whoa," she whispered softly. "What was that?" She bent her head over and saw Henry from the waist up, the rest was wrapped in a blanket like a burrito. He had slept beside her all night long on the floor with Claire beside her in the bed. Wendy smiled.

She quietly maneuvered past him. The sound of her footsteps pattered across the floor. She proceeded to make her way through the chaos. That's when her eyes caught the scene of black smoke smoldering in the direction of Finger Bones' cabin from her bedroom window. Everything from the night before came flooding back. The sandy river banks and the flames of the fire that had seemed to talk whirled into her mind. She remembered the log cabin burning with orange, yellow, and red flames, shooting high into the night skies. And the smell of burning wood had mixed with her nostrils as she got a whiff of that horrible odor.

Wendy paced back and forth procrastinating about approaching the window she had stood at the night before. Finally, she neared it with thoughts of Finger Bones walking out of the flames. She recalled all he had told her. She knew her experience had been very real.

She turned away from the window. Claire and Henry were still asleep. She decided to go downstairs into the kitchen where her mom was cooking homemade blueberry pancakes. Wendy's stomach started growling loudly for food when the smell of them hit her nostrils. She loved steaming hot blueberry pancakes straight from the iron skillet.

Wendy picked up her fork jabbing the large pile. She twisted her fork until a good portion stuck. She then stuffed the pancakes, dripping with syrup, into her mouth. She closed her eyes and smiled as she chewed.

While Wendy took several more savoring mouthfuls of her pancakes, Mr. Winkelmann sat next to her reading the Bridgeville Clipper newspaper. He read it religiously every morning after his breakfast while he finished his coffee. After reading the front page, her dad flipped the paper to the back. Wendy picked up her orange juice. She was drinking it when she noticed the front page of the Clipper. A large picture covered the top portion of the page. It was a picture of Finger Bones' cabin engulfed in flames. Her brain began churning. Before realizing what she had blurted, she said, "Dad, Finger Bones is okay."

Mr. Winkelmann was not an unkind or impatient man. He was serious most of the time and able to persevere in times of difficulty. In addition to his serious side, he had a warm compassionate side to him. He could talk to people. He had to communicate and talk to all different kinds of people in his line of work. Wendy thought he was good at what he did.

But when it came to talking to her, sometimes, she knew he wasn't one to say much. If he did speak, a grumble was always uttered with the remark. Not an angry grumble, one saying, "I'd rather you talk to your mom. She will know what to say." Then he would turn a raised eyebrow to her mom, hoping she'd take over the conversation.

He put the newspaper down on the table beside him. Mr. Winkelmann carefully chose his words. "I know you have questions, Wendy. Your mother, and I, will discuss this matter with you tonight. Do you understand?"

"But Dad, I don't have questions, I'm *telling* you Finger Bones *is* okay."

"Don't you mean to ask me *if* Finger Bones is okay?"

"No sir, I said Finger Bones *is* okay."

Mr. and Mrs. Winkelmann looked at each other with gloomy faces. Neither one knew how to tell their daughter the horrible news. Finger Bones was gone and he would not return.

Her mother walked over and sat on the other side of Wendy. "Oh Wendy, yes, Finger Bones is okay. But he is no longer with us. He's now in a peaceful place where he can rest."

"Oh, he'll be back!" she said, jabbing a piece of the pancake and twirling it in some syrup. "Soon he'll be smiling and carrying that stick of his with the sack. You wait and see. We have unfinished business to do. He has to come back."

Her father stared at her in bewilderment. He leaned toward his daughter. "What do you mean, Pumpkin, you have unfinished business?" Wendy's father called her 'Pumpkin' when he was tuned in to what she was saying.

"Finger Bones *and I* have unfinished work to do Dad. Oh, I don't know all the details about the job. But I do know he'll be back."

"Really and how do you know this?"

Wendy placed her fork down making a clank on her plate. She was annoyed with the questions. She looked straight into her dad's eyes and said, "Because Finger Bones told me so right after he walked out of the fire, that's how."

Her parents sat stunned. Before they could collect themselves, Claire and Henry came bouncing into the kitchen hollering, "Pancakes, we love your blueberry pancakes!"

Claire jumped and dropped down into a chair. Henry ran in behind her taking a flying leap, landing dead center in his chair. Both were jabbering and ready to eat. Wendy joined her two best friends. They yelled and chattered with joy over the wonderful morning only kids could have.

***

The morning sun could be felt beaming down as Wendy, Claire, and Henry ran through the backyard. They ran skipping and flipping and rolling down the small hills. Wendy told them to follow her. So they made their way through the woods that led to Bone River.

"I love it out here today. It's not too hot and not too cold. It is *just* right," Claire said.

Stopping at the edge of the woods, the three sat on a large fallen tree. They swung their legs and watched the river not more than twenty feet ahead of them.

"Why did you bring us down here, Wendy?" Henry asked.

"I wanted to talk without Mom and Dad listening to what I had to tell you. I knew if they heard they would start asking me a horde of questions again," Wendy said, rolling her eyes. "Plus, I wanted to tell you about Finger Bones."

Henry jerked his head toward Wendy. "What about Finger Bones?"

"Is he okay?" Claire asked. "Was he burned badly?"

Wendy looked down at her swinging legs. "Yes. He's okay. And no, he wasn't burned."

"Where is Finger Bones?" Henry stopped swinging his legs and looked all around. "Is he here?"

"I bet he's in the hospital, isn't he?" Claire asked.

Henry jumped from the trunk of the tree. "Can we go see him? If he's at the Bridgeville General Hospital we can ride our bikes."

Claire and Henry were rattling on so fast Wendy had to holler to stop them. "Claire and Henry, stop talking! He's not here right now."

"Well then where did he go?" Henry asked.

"He had to go away for a while. But he'll be back again soon. He said so. He said, 'I'll be back again soon enough.'"

"How did you talk to him if he wasn't here in Bridgeville?" Henry asked puzzled. "Did you go see him?" He narrowed his eyes. "Or did he come to see you last night after we went to sleep? You could've woken us up."

"I kind of went to see him. He told me all about what he did here in Bridgeville for many, many years. He did a special job. And now it's my turn." With more determination she said, "But he's going to return. He must return. He said someone upstairs wasn't finished with him down here and it's the reason he'll be back soon."

Claire and Henry cocked an eyebrow and looked at Wendy as though she had lost her mind.

Wendy decided she would have to prove them wrong. She knew she had talked to Finger Bones and she knew how to prove it to her best friends. Find the trunk.

"Listen, I know it sounds crazy and you've got questions. I can't explain it all right now, but I'm telling the truth," Wendy said. "Listen, Finger Bones told me a trunk has been hidden somewhere nearby. Finding it will prove I'm telling the truth. Will you help me find it?"

Claire and Henry looked at each other.

"Give me a chance," Wendy pleaded.

They nodded their heads in agreement and turned to Wendy.

"All you had to do is ask, Wendy," Claire said. "What you say may sound loopy, but through thick and thin we're friends till the end."

Henry shrugged his shoulders. "Sure, why not. What do you want us to do?"

Chapter Eight

Wendy skipped toward Henry, grabbing and hugging him. "Thank you so much, Henry."

She then turned and gave Claire a hug. "And you too, Claire. "

"Okay, you're welcome," she said with her cheeks turning red. "Now, um, let go. You're choking me."

Wendy let go and started, "First we are to search for a large black rock." She walked over and looked under an old, dead log. "It'll be found under wood. Finger Bones told me the rock originally came from England. He said on one side of the black rock we'd find a fossil of a scarab beetle, and when we found it, we would know it."

"Can the trunk be found under any kind of wood?" Claire asked.

"I should think so. Finger Bones didn't say. So I assume any kind of wood. I know it has been hidden in this area." Wendy bent over and flipped a large branch lying in the sand. A few bugs scuttled out running.

The three friends were at an area called, *River Rock*, located on Bone River. River Rock stretched a hundred yards in length, and the width went from one side of the river to the other. The deepest part was eight inches deep. Wendy, Claire, and Henry could walk across without any problem searching for the special rock.

All three sat on the bank of the river and hurriedly took off their socks and shoes. They rolled up their pants, jumped up, and went scurrying around in the sand like squirrels. They overturned logs and branches on both sides of the river. After flipping almost every piece of wood in sight, Claire and Henry were ready to throw in the towel. Wendy dragged her feet to the fallen tree they had been sitting on earlier. All three plopped down on it.

"Well we're back where we started," Claire said.

"What do we do now?" Henry asked. "We've turned over every single thing around here and all we have found were some love bugs and a few mosquitoes."

"Are you sure you heard correctly?" Claire lightly swatted Wendy on her leg. "You know how you half-way listen sometimes when someone is talking. Maybe he said to look somewhere else."

Wendy didn't answer. Looking serious, she took out a piece of bubblegum from her pocket and plopped it in her mouth. Wendy began thinking about what to do next. But before an idea surfaced, she heard a cracking sound. The three friends felt a shift of the old tree.

"Aaahh!" All three plummeted to the ground with a wallop.

"Are you two okay?" Wendy asked, sitting up and slapping the sand from her shorts.

"I'm fine I guess." Henry lay on his back. He slowly turned his head to one side. His eyes went wide when he saw several pieces of large concrete and wood close to his head.

"Look at this," he said stupefied. "Do you see this concrete? This stuff is thick. Three more inches and my head could have been pulverized."

"My rumpus took a good smack." Claire said, crawling to her knees. When she could manage she stood up, staggering in the rubble.

"Ouch. Hey Claire, will you help me?" Wendy asked, sitting among a pile of debris. "My rear hit something hard too, and it hurts."

"Tell me about it," Claire said, rubbing her bottom. She bobbled over, secured her footing, and stretched her hand out for Wendy to grab.

Wendy gripped Claire's hand. When she pushed up off the ground with her other hand, Wendy's eyes went wide. "Wait!" she exclaimed. "Let go, Claire." Wendy quickly scooted to one side and looked down. Underneath the many pieces of wood laid a black shiny object. "I see something. Help me," Wendy said eagerly.

All three dropped to their knees eagerly throwing wood pieces and chunks of concrete over their shoulders and out to the side. They then dug down and around the black object. Finally, the three wiggled the rock free.

Wendy grabbed the rock on both sides and flipped it over. In the center of it was the fossil of the scarab beetle.

"Awesome rock!" Henry exclaimed.

"It's pretty," Claire said.

Wendy traced her fingers over the fossil. She could feel the different segments of the beetle's body and see the insect's legs. An emerald color glimmered portraying the color of the living beetle.

Henry made a step forward. "Okay, back up." Henry bent over and lifted the ancient black rock.

"Can you handle toting the rock?" Claire asked.

"Stop worrying. I got this. Look at these guns," he said, gesturing toward his arms.

Claire rolled her eyes.

He heaved up the rock and turned toward Wendy. "Where do we go from here?"

"Now we need to find a large, odd shaped, stone. Finger Bones told me the rock fits in a slot at the top of the stone. It's in this area too. The fossil of the scarab beetle should fit perfectly face down in the hole. The rock will act like a key, opening the secret compartment. In the hidden compartment, we'll find the trunk."

Wendy and Claire went to work looking for the perfect stone. Running and splashing, they plunged along in the water. The coolness of it tickled their ankles and feet.

Henry followed carrying the black rock snug against his chest. Several places were found. But a perfect fit it was not. All three crossed over to the other side of the river. Sand was kicked and holes were dug as they combed every log and rock.

Wendy and Henry spotted some bushes to search and began walking toward them. Claire decided to go the other way and wade back across River Rock. She told them she wanted to dry her feet and put her shoes back on. She said was tired. Wendy knew she was worried about catching a cold.

As Claire made her way back across the river she turned her head and hollered, "You two better be careful over there. Anything could live in those bushes."

She then whirled her head back around and before she knew what happened rammed her big toe into something in the middle of the river. "Aaahh," Claire shrieked. She fell sprawling and landed into the river face first. She pushed herself up in sitting position and grabbed her toe. "Where did this dang humongous stone come from?" she screamed, slapping the top of the stone with her other hand. "It wasn't here before...or ever."

"Stone, she said stone," Henry said, turning excited. "Stay right where you are Claire. And don't move."

"Oh, I'm getting out of this water, Henry. It's freezing! I'm wet and cold and..."

"Oh, no you're not, Missy!" Wendy plunged through the bushes running. "Don't you dare move, Claire Grace Clark. And keep your hand on that stone. We're on our way."

Wendy and Henry sprinted through the shallow river. Water splashed in their faces as they rushed toward Claire. When they reached the middle, Wendy and Henry stood staring at the enormous stone.

"Where did it come from?" Henry asked.

Claire sat next to the stone with her hand plopped on top of it. "How do I know?" Claire spat. "Well is there a hole in the top?

"Hang on," Wendy said.

"Gosh, I hope so. I have to get some satisfaction out of getting sopping wet. I'll probably get a cold for sure now."

"Oh, pipe down and let me look," Wendy said, stepping up to it. She whispered as though she didn't want anyone to hear. "There's a hole in the top. I can't tell if the rock will fit though." Wendy spoke louder. "Henry, see if the rock fits."

Henry waded over and lifted the rock in ready position. He then lowered and placed the rock into the stone. Henry heard, and then felt, a click. "Oh wow, oh wow," Henry said. "It's a perfect fit. Now what?"

"Uh, well it's supposed to open up or reveal where the trunk is concealed," Wendy said, shrugging her shoulder.

Henry leaned over the stone and listened. "Nothing is happening."

"Wait, give it a little longer," Wendy said. "Maybe it takes a moment or two. Be patient."

Sure enough, soon the stone started turning red hot and the water around it began to boil. A muffled rumbling was heard. It became louder and louder.

Claire thought she felt the ground shake. She then jumped up and started to panic. "Whoa, guys, move it! The grounds moving! And it's getting hot in here!"

The three took off splashing through the water. At the bank of the river, Wendy hit the ground followed by Claire and

Henry. They turned and gazed as the water boiled and churned. Hot bubbles gurgled and splattered causing steam to rise into the air. Finally, the stone immersed and sank under the water.

Then without warning, an enormous explosion sounded behind them. All three ducked and covered their heads while lying on the ground. Wendy held her head up and peeked. The remainder of the large tree trunk was flying all over the place along with pieces of concrete.

"Yikes, what's happening?" Henry yelled over the clamor of rocks, wood, stone, and sand flying in all directions.

"Stay down, let's wait until it's over before we jump up," Wendy hollered.

"Don't you worry, I'm not moving. I don't know if I could if I wanted to," Claire said, her voice shaking.

Wendy and Claire lay still until all the debris had stopped falling and the water stopped boiling in River Rock. Henry remained on the ground as well. Wendy could tell by the twitch in his leg, Henry wanted to run.

At last, everything came to a halt. All was quiet. The moment seemed to last forever. Guardedly, Wendy and her friends got up and looked around.

Wendy was the first to approach where the tree trunk had laid. Claire and Henry walked up behind her. No one said anything. They stared at the trunk in front of them.

"The entire time the trunk was right under us," Wendy said.

Wendy noticed the large rusty chains wrapped around the trunk. The chains were secured with a large lock. The trunk had sat on a concrete slab. Concrete and asphalt, covered with sand, had been the top of the compartment. The blast had blown the seal into some nearby trees. The walls of the compartment were scattered all over the place.

Henry was the one who finally moved. He shook his head and stepped forward. He took hold of the lock and gave it a jerk. "Hey, um, Wendy, do you have the key?"

"No, Finger Bones didn't say anything about a key. He told me to find the black rock and find the slot it fit in to open the secret compartment. After that, I have no idea."

A fist size piece of concrete lay half submerged in the sand. Claire reached over to grab it. "Look how thick this concrete is. Finger Bones must be hiding something special in that trunk."

"Yeah," Henry said with wide eyes.

Claire dropped the concrete. It landed in the sand with a thud. "Well, we need to drag it back to Wendy's house. Then the three of us can find a way to open to this ancient thing."

"Okay, let's see if we can drag it," Wendy said. "We can put the trunk in my tree house using the pulley."

Wendy, Claire, and Henry grabbed one end of the chain. They heaved the trunk off the concrete slab and through the sand. The sand beneath their feet gave way as they heaved and pulled it. After only five or six feet, they couldn't pull any more.

"Whoa, it's way too heavy," Claire said.

"Come on, we can do this," Wendy encouraged.

Claire and Henry looked at each other and then back at Wendy.

Wendy looked back at them. Claire had strings of sweat rolling down both temples and she was breathing heavy. Henry's long bangs were glued to his forehead.

Wendy reached in her pocket. Lightening the mood she said, "Ha, see I'm smart. I put the gum in a zip lock bag." All three laughed. Wendy tossed a piece of bubblegum to Claire and Henry. "Now, let me think."

While Wendy thought, Claire and Henry looked all around the trunk.

"Wow, this is the coolest trunk I have ever seen!" Henry exclaimed.

"I can't wait to see what's in it," Claire said, raising her eyebrows.

"How are we going to get this heavy thing all the way to the tree house? We need more muscle," Henry said.

"Oh my, that's it!" Wendy exclaimed.

"What?" Claire and Henry asked at the same time.

"We can make a stretcher. It'll be ideal to pull it. Henry, remember your brother's Boy Scout manual? We read it in his room during the summer. We learned how to make a stretcher from two strong branches, a rope, and a blanket."

"Oh yeah, I remember. We pulled each other around for days on that thing."

Wendy shook a finger at him. "And if you recall, Henry, we used it when we helped your dad clean out that garage."

"I still have the branches in the garage. I know exactly where I left them. We could carry the trunk with no problem. I hid the branches in the garage under some blankets with the water skis. I'm good at hiding stuff. I knew nobody would find them with the water skis," he said proudly.

"You go get the branches, Henry. Claire and I will run and grab one of the old sheets from my room. Dad has some rope in the garage."

"Okay, let's make a stretcher and get this trunk to the tree house," Henry said. "I want to find out what's inside this thing too."

***

Wendy, Claire, and Henry towed the trunk on the stretcher through the sand, up the hill, and down the path. It took another hour for the three to connect it to the pulley, carefully lift it, and put it in the tree house.

All three plopped down hassling on the floor of the big tree house. Their backs were propped against the walls and their feet propped against the trunk. They were exhausted and in no hurry to move. For a long while, Wendy, Claire, and Henry sat staring and wondering what was on the inside of the mysterious trunk.

Chapter Nine

"I think he left behind a pirate's treasure box. Don't you remember all those stories about Finger Bones stashing treasure under his bed?" Henry asked the girls.

"Uh, no Henry, those stories about the treasure were about an old man who hoarded his money," Claire said. "His name was Abner Grapples. Remember, Buck Fergus and his two goons, Paul Ward and Duke Gideon? They claimed Finger Bones was the one who hid children under his bed in a dungeon."

"Oh yeah, that's the way it goes."

"All I know is what Dad told me about Mr. Grapples," Wendy said. "Dad said Mr. Grapples drowned in Bone River during the flood."

"My brother, Tom, said Mr. Grapples was the meanest man who ever walked the earth, and was the stingiest man to ever live in Bridgeville," Henry said. "He had to write a paper on Abner Grapples in his English class. Tom's in the tenth grade and he said they have to write a lot of papers."

"Yeah, I heard Mr. Grapples was a mean man and he cared more about himself than he did his own wife," Claire said, propping her hands on her hips. "You know, Mrs. Maple Jean, the lady who lives across the street from us? My grandmother was telling her the other day, when Grandmother and she were having their weekly gripe session; she said Mr. Grapples treated his wife like one of his fancy paintings."

"Sure did. He was always paying lots of money for those things. And he expected her to act like one of his expensive paintings too. He wanted her to dress perfect and act perfect in front of his so called friends. But then his wife became sick in the winter of..."

"The year was 1937," Claire said. "I know because I heard Grandmother tell Mrs. Jean about it." She tapped her head. "And I have a good memory."

"I remember now. Todd had that part written in his paper. I'm sure I would've remembered it if someone would have given me a second to think," he bellyached, glancing at Claire.

"Oh good grief, tell the story," Claire snapped.

"Anyway, it was 1937 and Mrs. Grapples got real sick," Henry continued. "She stayed in bed and stared straight ahead at a picture of her and her husband. That's all she did for the last two weeks of her life. Why the old geezer had more money than anyone alive, I would guess, and he wouldn't allow for a single doctor to help her."

"I heard Grandmother tell Mrs. Maple Jean one more thing I found interesting," Claire said. "Abner Grapples ran for mayor of the town after his wife passed. But he lost. Grandmother said Grapples was mean before he ran for mayor. But when he lost, she said that man grew meaner. He thought his money would buy that position, but he was wrong.

Wendy pursed out her lips and scrunched her face. She was getting madder by the minute at this man she never met.

"As the years went by Abner Grapples stopped spending his money and started hoarding it," Claire said. "He felt if he didn't deserve to be mayor, the townspeople didn't deserve his money. Many people have told through the years old Grapples began to hide his money in a cave on Bone River. Bunches of people have hunted for the cave the last one hundred years. But until this day, no one has found it."

"You know, it has been said the notorious Lefty Lennie Spinsters worked for old man Grapples and helped him stash the money, and treasures." Henry said. "Locals have said he also robbed for Grapples, however, it was never proven."

"To rob is bad. For him to treat his wife so terribly is even worse," Wendy said, narrowing her eyes. "Grapples should have taken better care of his wife. I expect he died a lonely man being so mean."

"You got that right," Henry said flatly. "Not one person from Bridgeville was at his gravesite but the grave diggers."

Wendy changed the subject. "Well, there's *no* pirate's treasure in the trunk, Henry. But do know the items inside are valuable. Finger Bones said so. And when I figure out how to unlock this trunk, we can all see the treasure inside. But for now, I think we need to go and refuel. It's time to eat."

"I agree one hundred percent," Henry said, patting his stomach.

"Oh, me too! I definitely think my tank needs refueling," Claire agreed, giggling.

"Last one inside the house is a rotten egg," Henry shouted, hurrying down the tree house ladder. Wendy and Claire jumped up and scuttled down the ladder close behind him.

***

"We're hungry!" Wendy and Claire and Henry rushed inside yelling.

"Are we having hotdogs today, Mrs. Winkelmann?" Claire asked.

"Oh wow, I hope so. Those are the bomb!" Henry said happily.

Mrs. Winkelmann pointed her index finger in the air. "Wait a minute. Yes, we are having hotdogs. But first, all three of you march straight into that bathroom and wash your hands all the way up to those dirty elbows of yours before you sit at this table."

"Yes mam!" The three yelled in unison, while marching to the bathroom sink.

Mr. Winkelmann came in the back door as Wendy, Claire, and Henry marched back into the kitchen and sat down at the table. "Well, hello guys," Mr. Winkelmann said, squirting soap on his hands. "What have you three been up to all morning?"

The three looked at Mr. Winkelmann with guilty faces. Not a word was uttered.

"Hum, no one's talking? I hope you three are staying out of trouble," he said, trying to sound serious. He grabbed a towel and dried his hands. He turned to the three sitting at the table. "I would hate to carry you downtown and lock you up for mischief."

"Oh, no sir, we for sure don't need to go downtown," Henry said, smiling, raising his eyebrows. "We're definitely doing something good." Henry took a huge bite and stuffed his mouth with his hotdog. "Why, if anyfing, we are helfing Briff-fille."

"Oh you are? And how are you helping Bridgeville, Henry?"

"Well sir," Henry began, but paused to swallow the food. "We're..."

"We're staying out of trouble, Dad. How else could a kid help its town? I mean, jeez, we're just kids!" Wendy blurted, giving Henry narrowed eyes.

Mr. Winkelmann lightly laughed as he picked up his hotdog shifting it in his fingers. "Well excellent, as long as you are helping Bridgeville, I can't complain."

"Wendy, when you finish eating you and I are driving into town. I have some errands to do this morning. Your father will go back to work," Mrs. Winkelmann said as she brought over fresh cut French fries to go with the hotdogs.

"Claire, your grandmother called. And Henry, your mother called too. Both said to come home when you have finished eating. You both have chores to do. Claire, you also have piano lessons late this afternoon."

"Toilet duty at my house," Claire complained, slowing on her chewing. "Then the dreaded piano lessons with Mrs. Pittman."

"Trash duty at my house," Henry grumbled. "Tom always has football practice or some important football training. I have to do his chores too."

"Oh, I'm sure you'll both survive," Mrs. Winkelmann said reassuringly.

The look on Henry's face as he took another bite of his hotdog said he wasn't convinced he would survive.

Chapter Ten

Wendy decided she would go to the Bridgeville Pubic Library while her mother ran errands in town. She hadn't spoken with Mrs. Taylor or Mrs. Harper since Finger Bones went away. She knew the sisters were probably upset and she wanted to check on them.

Mrs. Winkelmann parked between the police station and library. Wendy looked out of the car window and saw the bench where Finger Bones and she had sat many times. It felt eerie not seeing Finger Bones contentedly sitting on the old wooden bench, smiling his blissful smile.

"Wendy, you stay at the library and don't go wandering around. I'll come get you when I'm finished, okay?"

"Yes ma'am," Wendy murmured. She got out of the car and walked up to the unoccupied bench. Wendy sat down and placed her hand on the spot where Finger Bones used to sit. She thought about the last time they had sat together on the bench.

Wendy slowly turned her head and looked down at her hand. She then raised her head and pretended to look at Finger Bones sitting beside her. She imagined him eating his fruit and making his banana sandwiches as he sat talking to her.

Wendy felt as though a frog had been jammed in her throat. "He did love his snacks," she said out loud with her eyes full of tears.

While Wendy sat and reminisced about the happy times they had shared on the bench, she started getting a knot in her stomach. More tears emerged and flowed down her cheeks. "Finger Bones, you need to come back now. I miss you. You hear me? You did say you would return. We've got unfinished business here in Bridgeville. That's what you said. I heard you. You said, 'we have unfinished business is what we have and we are to do it together.'"

Wendy sniffled. She took in a deep breath, stood, and walked to the library. With pouting lips, she walked aimlessly through the doors.

Mrs. Taylor was placing books on the shelf in the romance section when she spotted Wendy. Mrs. Taylor's sister, Mrs. Harper, was helping her today. Mrs. Taylor tapped her sister on the shoulder and nodded toward Wendy. They set the books they carried on the book cart. Mrs. Taylor waved her hand in the air to get Wendy's attention.

Wendy wiped the tears from her face, but more surfaced. They streamed down her cheeks. She walked to where the sisters stood. "I came to see you, Mrs. Taylor, and look at me," Wendy said, wiping her eyes. I'm glad to see you too, Mrs. Harper. I rode to town with Mom. She said for me to stay here until she finishes what she has to do in town."

Mrs. Taylor stepped up first and gave Wendy a hug. "Sister and I are happy to see you."

"Yes we are. How are you doing, dear?" Mrs. Harper asked, giving Wendy a hug.

"I'm okay I guess. Or I was until I saw the bench Finger Bones and I sat at so many times together. Then my stomach started feeling funny and I began to doubt what he had said."

The sisters looked at each other.

Mrs. Harper then looked at Wendy. "Wendy, what did Finger Bones say?" she said, pulling a chair out for both to sit. Mrs. Taylor sat with them.

"He said we had unfinished business to do here in Bridgeville. My dad didn't seem to believe me when I told him. But it's the truth," Wendy said defensively. "Finger Bones said he would be back soon."

Mrs. Taylor bent over and took Wendy by the hands. She looked Wendy in the eyes. "Sister and I believe you," she said sincerely.

"Yes we do," Mrs. Harper said. "And Wendy, if you need to talk to anyone about anything, Mrs. Taylor and I will listen. We will help in anyway."

Wendy wiped more tears. "Thanks."

"You are very welcome. Just promise to come to us if you need anything. And we mean…anything."

"I promise," Wendy said. "I'm just going to go read until Mom gets here." Wendy stood and headed to the kid's section of books.

She browsed a row of books. Wendy didn't really look closely at them. Pulling one from the shelf, she turned and moped over to the nearest table. She slumped in a chair and flipped open the book.

"Why do you have such a long face, Wendy?" asked a familiar male voice.

Wendy looked up, but no one was there. She wiped the tears from her face with the back of her hands and sniffed. She turned around to see if someone was standing behind her. But no one was there either. "Hey, who said that?"

"Down here, look down here! In the book, look at the book."

Slowly Wendy bent her head. She couldn't believe what she saw. On page 72 of the book was a picture of a room, and in the room was a full length mirror. Standing smack in the middle of the full length mirror was none other than, Finger Bones!

"It's you, oh it's truly you!" Wendy said, wiping her nose with the sleeve of her jacket. "Yuck, I'm sorry. Gross, I know." She grabbed some tissue from the tissue box on the table. "I was so sad, Finger Bones. Just a while ago on our bench I was miserable. You were not there when Mom and I pulled up to park the car. And I got this knot in my stomach I had never felt before. I began thinking about all the times we sat and talked. I thought about how we met and how I was not scared of you anymore. And then I thought about you eating a banana sandwich."

Finger Bones smiled a tender-hearted smile. "Don't cry, little Wendy. I am here. I said I would come back. I had to take care of some other business before returning. But I'm here to stay for as long as you need me now."

Wendy wiped the tears from her eyes again with the tissue. She tried to stop the fresh tears from flowing. "Good. I will need you for a good long time so don't go far again."

"Okay, I won't go far." Finger Bones smiled. He had an idea. "Hey, I have something I know will cheer you up and will help you feel better." He held up an object on a long string. "See this? It's a whistle Wendy. Now anytime you need me, you blow this whistle and I will come to wherever you are." Amazingly, out of the page Finger Bones stretched his arm with the whistle in his hand. "Here, take this and place it around your neck. When you need me blow the whistle. No one will hear but me."

Wendy took hold of the whistle on the string. "Can I try it now?" she asked, placing the string around her neck.

"Well sure you can. Let's give it a test run. I'll pop away and you blow the whistle. When I hear the sound, I will pop back into the mirror. Okay?"

Wendy slowly placed the whistle in her mouth. But then decided she would count to five before blowing it. She removed the whistle and counted in a whispered voice. "One, two, three, four, and five..." She blew as hard as she could, but not a sound was made. She could feel the little ball inside the whistle jiggle and vibrate like her P.E. coach's whistle. Yet this whistle didn't make a noise.

"Hello there, little missy," Finger Bones announced. He popped back in the mirror right at the moment she blew. "Hee-hee, see it works."

Wendy laughed with him. She was already feeling much better than she did earlier. And her feeling better helped her to remember about the trunk. "Oh yes, Finger Bones. I wanted to tell you we found the trunk this morning. It's now in my tree house. But it's locked and we can't open it. Do you have a key?"

Finger Bones pulled a chain full of keys from his pocket. He detached one large key from the pile. Again, stretching his arm from the page he held out the key for Wendy to take. "Here you go my little friend. This key will open the trunk. Attach it to the string with the whistle."

Wendy clutched the key in her hand and maneuvered it until it was on the string.

"Good. Now, be careful with the contents. You need to make certain your two friends understand the importance of what's inside and they should be careful as well. We wouldn't want an accident to happen, or worse, not have the needed ingredients when our unfinished business comes around."

"I'll talk to them Finger Bones. They've been wonderful about everything so far. I know they will be just as cautious."

Chapter Eleven

Henry rolled on the tree house floor. Clasped against his chest, he held a tied bag marked SALT. Engraved above the word was an alchemy symbol, which consisted of a circle with a horizontal line through the middle.

"You've got to be kidding me. You mean to tell me Finger Bones popped up in a full-length mirror on page 72 in a book? He talked to you and gave you the whistle around your neck? He then handed you a key while in the book? Did I get all of this right?" He sat up, raised his arms, and held up the bag. "Now you have opened this special and important trunk and this was what was in it? What else can we find in this trunk? I've got to see this!" he exclaimed, scooting to the trunk on his knees, giggling so hard he almost choked.

"Stop it." Wendy slapped his hand, grabbed the bag of salt, and said, "I did see Finger Bones. And when Claire gets back from her piano lessons in just a few minutes, I'll show you how the whistle works. Until then, hands off the trunk. Do you hear me?"

"Okay, okay, don't get so edgy," he said, calming down his laughter and throwing up his hands. "It's just...I mean...you know...salt." He looked at Wendy, bit his bottom lip, and looked away from her glaring eyes. He stayed quiet until Claire got back from her lessons.

Wendy and Henry heard Claire climbing up the stairs a few minutes later. Actually, they heard her when she was jogging across the yard yelling, "Here I come. I'm almost at the ladder. Now I am climbing the ladder. I'm opening the door."

"Yes, we can see you are, Claire. Hurry and close the trap door," Wendy said. "We don't want anyone to hear what I have to say or see what I have to show you."

Claire closed the door and sat next to Wendy. "What is it?" Claire asked. She looked at Henry strangely.

"Yeah, it's *so* amazing," Henry said, rolling his eyes and starting to snicker again.

Wendy narrowed her eyes and tightened her lips. "Okay, that's it." She yanked the whistle out hanging on the string, grabbed the whistle, and blew it as hard as she could blow.

"Now that *is* an important item there, Wendy, a whistle with no sound," Henry said sarcastically.

Wendy didn't comment on Henry's remark. Instead, a smile spread over her face.

Claire, she had a different look. It was shock. Claire reached over and grabbed Wendy by the shirt. She struggled to suck in air, but the air blocked in her throat.

"What? What is it?" Henry asked, grinning,

Claire pointed to something behind Henry. And something behind Henry suddenly breathed on his neck

"Boo," said a familiar voice.

Henry jumped in one leap over to the other side of the tree house beside Wendy and Claire. His mouth fell wide open and his heart beat so fast he thought it would burst from his chest. And when he focused on who had startled him, his eyes went wide.

"What's the matter, Henry? Didn't you think it was funny?" Wendy asked giggling.

Henry didn't respond to Wendy's question. He headed straight for the trap door. She knew his legs were saying run and he would, if he could get through the trap door.

Claire was still in her same position. She was too scared to move, or to cry. So she sat and stared a stupefied stare. Wendy had to make a move.

"Snap out of it, Claire!" Wendy hollered, rushing toward Henry. "Help me grab him. It's just Finger Bones. He's not going to hurt us. He's here to help us."

Claire came to her senses, shook her head, and helped Wendy seize Henry. Finally, all three settled down. "Now sit still, Henry," Wendy demanded. "You're *not* going through the door until I say what I have to say. Then if you still think you need to run, I'll open the trap door for you."

Wendy could tell he was still not convinced, but he sat down. He pulled his unbuttoned jacket around him and held it tightly. His eyes did not stray from Finger Bones.

Finger Bones sat Indian style on the floor with Wendy and her two best friends. He stayed quiet for the time being allowing Wendy to talk.

"Finger Bones told me about a job the night of the fire. He said there was a special job to be done in Bridgeville. And this trunk holds all the tools and necessities we will need to continue the work."

"Are you listening, Henry?" Wendy asked, already irritated at him.

Henry's eyes did not blink. "Sure, I heard every word you said. You said Finger Bones came to you the night of the fire. He told you about the job which had to be done in Bridgeville. And the trunk holds all the stuff we need."

"Then why are you staring at Finger Bones? Are you afraid of ghosts or something?"

"Or something," Henry answered.

Wendy followed Henry's gaze and figured it out. She gave a small smile. Propped up against the tree house wall behind Finger Bones was the famous stick with the burlap bag. "It's okay, Henry. You can stop staring a hole through it. No kids are trapped in the bag and he's not here to capture us. The stories aren't true." She looked over at Finger Bones. "Finger Bones carries ingredients, and sometimes a banana sandwich and an apple in the sack."

"She's correct," Finger Bones said, smiling with a twinkle in his eye. He slapped his knee and looked at Henry. "Hee-hee, why Henry, you look as though you've seen a ghost. You're as white as an albino opossum."

Wendy giggled and looked at Henry. Then all went quiet. It seemed an eternity before Henry's color surfaced.

"Finger Bones don't look like a ghost," Henry said, looking from the burlap sack to Finger Bones. Becoming bolder, Henry narrowed his eyes and crossed his arms. "In fact, Finger Bones looks alive and kicking,"

"Well, you're turning from scared to bold mighty fast," Wendy said.

"Ah, Henry, you are skeptical about me being a ghost, aren't you?" Finger Bones asked intrigued.

"I'm just saying."

"Yes you are and I can see it written all over your face. I guess I'm going to have to show you," he said, shaking his finger. "Okay, come here."

Henry stood and walked toward Finger Bones. Finger Bones stood.

Henry lightly poked the old ghost in the stomach with his finger. "I can see you and I can touch you. That doesn't show me anything. I thought ghosts floated up-and-down and could go through things, like doors."

"Back-up and watch closely," Finger Bones said. To add to the moment, Finger Bones raised his right hand and touched the brim of his hat. Suddenly, a puff of smoke emerged and surrounded Finger Bones. The smoke grew thicker until engulfing him completely. When the smoke cleared, Finger Bones still sat in his same position. He sat smiling his broad smile.

Henry's eyes grew wide and Claire and Wendy's mouths dropped open, and for good reason. Sitting before them was an amazing sight. Finger Bones looked different. The three could see right through him. He glowed. Sparkles flew from his body with each movement. And to top it off, Finger Bones floated about three inches from the floor.

"Do I look like a ghost now, Henry?"

"Uh huh, I would say you look exactly like a ghost," he said with eyes bulging again.

"Go ahead and give it a try," Finger Bones said, patting his belly.

Henry stretched out his arm and poked Finger Bones in the belly. But Henry's hand did not stop at Finger Bones' stomach. Henry's hand continued going forward through Finger Bones middles and out his back!

Henry wiggled his fingers. "Oh wow! Cool, look at this! I can see my hand on the other side and my arm is still going through his insides!"

"Ew gross, I see it, Henry," Claire said with a scrunched up nose.

"I told you he was a ghost, Henry!" Wendy blurted. Wendy was actually amazed at the sight too, though she tried not to show it.

"Okay, I believe you," Henry said. He pulled his arm back and rubbed his fingers and hands. He sat down.

Claire grabbed a rag from a shelf in the tree house. "Take this and wipe your hands. You may have gotten some kind of weird ghost stuff on you or something."

Once again another cloud of smoke encircled Finger Bones. He returned to his former appearance.

"It's time to get down to business." Finger Bones squatted and placed both hands on top of the trunk. "It is very important to know and understand what the contents of the trunk are used for and what to do with the ingredients."

Wendy, Claire, and Henry settled down to listen.

"Wendy was chosen for an important job to do right here in Bridgeville. The special stick made of birch chose her," Finger Bones said, turning and grabbing the stick. "As I told Wendy, this is the one of the many jobs the stick has. And the bag, it carries several necessities. Mostly, I carry the ingredients in it. But together, the stick and the burlap bag work together and are magical.

Wendy will be carrying her ingredients in backpacks. I will continue to tote the stick. Claire and Henry, will you help her in this special job?"

"What will we be doing? How can we help?" Claire asked.

"By learning the contents as Wendy learns you will help her catch and send ghosts on to their next destination."

"Do what?" Claire asked. She pushed back with her hands trying to make some distance from Finger Bones.

Henry sat straight up and his body began moving slightly up and down. The heebie-jeebies crawled down his spine. Once again, his brain was telling him to run.

"I'm j-just a kid," Claire stuttered. "I can't."

Wendy knew she had to say something and fast. "Henry, be still. Claire, Henry, I have a job to do and it's too big of a job for me to do by myself. I need you guys now more than ever. You both are my best friends. We may be kids, but together we can do this! Will you do it? Will you help me?"

"I was chosen many years ago and have protected the town for many years," Finger Bones said. "Now it's Wendy's turn. I will assist her, and the two of you also, if you choose to help. I will be here as long as you need me."

Henry looked at Claire. Claire stared back at Henry. After calming down, they looked at Wendy simultaneously saying, "Okay, we'll help you."

119

Wendy spit in her own hand. Claire and Henry spit in their hands. They all rubbed them together, and then slapped one hand on top of the other chanting, "Through thick and thin, during good times and bad, we are definitely best friends until the end."

"We are ready to open the trunk," Finger Bones said. He lifted the lid and reached into the trunk as he had many times before.

Chapter Twelve

"First we have salt," Finger Bones said, pulling out the bag and pointing to the word. There was a symbol above the word. It was a circle with a horizontal line through the middle. "Salt's used to fend off ghosts or prevent them from passing over into a certain area. I always kept a large supply when hunting. Salt helps to capture the ghosts. You take the salt and pour a solid line of it around the area you want to prevent the ghost from crossing over."

"And salt really works?" Henry asked. This time he was not laughing.

"Yes, the circle of salt is like a cage and prevents ghosts from passing the salt line. For Level One ghosts, the salt will do the job."

"What do you mean Level One ghosts?" Henry asked.

"There are three levels of ghosts. In time we will learn about all three levels. The salt will not hold Level Two or Level Three ghosts for long."

"Finger Bones, after we capture the ghosts how do we send them to their next destination?" Wendy asked quickly, changing the subject.

"Good question Wendy." Finger Bones carefully placed the salt back in its compartment and then reached to grab a different bag. This bag was about the same size as the salt bag.

"Aw yes, the Hotfoot Powder." Finger Bones turned the bag around and held it up so the three friends could see the word and symbol on it. "The triangle symbol symbolizes the word Hotfoot Powder. The symbol means fire. When we use the Hot Foot Powder it's kind of like fighting fire with fire." Finger Bones slightly shook the bag up and down.

"Don't shake it." Henry said, turning his head.

"Hee-hee, it's not going to blow up, Henry. You pour the Hot Foot Powder in a soda bottle after capturing a ghost along with the name of the ghost on a piece of paper. Next, you cork the bottle. Then you run to Bone River as fast as you can and throw the bottle to the middle of the river. If you follow these instructions you will send the ghost to his next destination as fast as lightning strikes."

"What all ingredients are in the Hotfoot Powder, Finger Bones?" Wendy asked. "I can feel and hear something crunching in the bag."

"Let me see," thought Finger Bones out loud. He lifted his finger to his chin. "The ingredients for Hot Foot Powder include cayenne pepper, black pepper, a little sea salt, and insect chitins."

"Ew, insect chitins?" Claire asked, crumpling up her nose.

"Yeah, remember we learned about insect chitins in science. It's the hard part, the exoskeleton," Henry said.

"Yes it is," Finger Bones said. "And all the ingredients mixed together can make a strong Hot Foot Powder." He placed the Hotfoot Powder bag back in the trunk.

"Now, I have one more item to show..."

"Wait, Finger Bones," Wendy interrupted. "I have a question. What are all these drawers on the side of the trunk?" Wendy pointed to several drawers. "Like this one, there's part of a plant sticking out from it."

Finger Bones opened the drawer where a long stemmed plant was placed. He delicately pulled out the plant. It had gray-green foliage and about a three inch beige-colored bloom on the tip. The flower was still fresh and in bloom. He lifted the flower up to his nose and pulled it from one end of the stem to the other under his nose, breathing in a large breath. "Aw, it smells of mints. I did love a hot cup of catnip before going to bed."

"Do we drink it?" Claire asked.

"Well, you can. I suggest buying the catnip from the store if you want to drink it though," Finger Bones said. "If swallowed by a ghost the catnip acts like a sedative, putting the meanest ghost to sleep right away like a baby kitten. Now, the trick's getting the ghost to swallow it." Fingers Bones winked an eye and placed the stem back in the drawer.

He then picked up a smaller, darker bag from the trunk. This particular bag contained a picture of a tombstone on it. Below the picture it read, Graveyard Dirt. "This special bag needs to be taken seriously. In this small bag we have dirt from a grave. And in this dirt is part of someone's soul."

"Part of their soul is *in* the dirt?" This time Wendy looked surprised with her big green eyes.

Claire breathed in sharply. She slapped a hand over her mouth.

Henry acted differently. "How cool! May I hold the bag?"

"Sure. Just be easy. Place one hand under the bag and grab with the other hand where it is tied, right here."

Henry lifted his arms and extended his hands, grasping the bag as he was told. "Awesome! Look Wendy and Claire.

I'm holding dirt from the grave of a dead person. And part of his *soul* fills the bag."

"Okay Henry, hand it here. We have to be extra careful with this one. It wouldn't be a good idea to drop it. I collected this special grave yard dirt a few hours before the cabin was burned. Finger Bones reached for the bag. Taking the bag, he looked from the bag to Wendy. "And this particular soul enslaved in this bag, Wendy Dee Winkelmann, is your first job."

Wendy scooted up on her knees to get a closer look. "Who is it Finger Bones?"

"The dirt in this bag is from the grave of none other than, Lefty Lenny Spinsters."

"Are you talking about the notorious mobster of Bridgeville who shot up The Bridgeville Jewel Box and frightened and terrorized many others?" Henry blurted in one breath. "He broke out of jail once and got away on a moving train!" Henry clasped his hands placing them on his head. "The dude is like a legend in this town!"

"The one and only," Finger Bones said with a solemn expression. "I'm afraid he's back. And whatever his reason, it's not a good one I'm sure of it. Your job is to find him and send him on to his next dwelling. He may not go easily, or voluntarily. Sometimes you have to send ghosts by force. But either way they have to go."

Without a word being uttered, Finger Bones set the bag into the old trunk. He then raised his arms grasping the lid, closing it shut.

"Lefty Lennie Spinsters is the ghost I saw at your cabin isn't he, Finger Bones?" Wendy asked.

"Yes Wendy, he is."

The mood in the tree house turned somber. Wendy gazed down at the wooden plank floors. She then raised her head and looked at Finger Bones. "Okay, what do we need to do first, Finger Bones? How do we find this ghost of Lefty Lennie Spinsters?"

"Listen closely, for every single mouthful I say is important," Finger Bones said, pointing to the three friends.

127

Wendy, Claire, and Henry sat shaking their heads up and down.

"Before hunting ghosts, first, write down everything told and taught to you. And I mean every word to the best of your recollection.

Next, all three of you need to secure this area where the trunk is kept. There are things you need to do to help prevent ghosts from entering the premises. Believe me. Someday, they will try to seize the trunk, or you.

Iron horseshoes above the doorway is a good preventative. Or hanging them against the walls inside will work. Find some garlic and line the walls, place plants of aloe around too. The aloe will guard against evil and prevent accidents ghosts are liable to make happen. Plus, if an accident does happen, the aloe will be close by to help heal cuts and scratches.

At your home you need to protect yourself. Supplies of wintergreen leaves inside the trunk are provided. Place the leaves under your pillow to protect yourself against any kind of evil that may be lurking. And you know the catnip growing all around outside your homes? As I said earlier, the catnip will put a ghost to sleep."

No one noticed the perplexed look which covered Claire's face until Finger Bones glanced her way. He raised an eyebrow. Claire stared at Finger Bones, but her mind was in a different place.

Henry caught Finger Bones' expression and followed his gaze to Claire. Henry reached over, grabbed Claire by the arms, and shook her. "Claire, Claire, come back to earth."

"What, Henry?"

"What are you thinking about? You act like you're in another world."

"Oh sorry, I was just thinking." She then began to look worried. "Finger Bones, you said you have hunted ghosts for years. Now, Wendy will take over the job."

"Yes, you are correct."

"And now you're a ghost."

"Yes."

"Finger Bones, um, were you murdered?" Claire asked almost fearful to hear the answer.

"Yes I was," Finger Bones said slowly, but honestly. "The ghosts responsible were hoping it would better their odds. By getting rid of me, they thought it might hinder us from helping ghosts go on to their next destination, and make it easier to keep more ghosts here in Bridgeville."

"That leads me to my main question. You said something like, 'We're here to do good for Bridgeville and to stop any evil lurking.'" Claire took a deep gulp and asked, "Is there an evil lurking, Finger Bones?"

Henry's eyes grew wide. He legs had that weird feeling again. He wanted to run.

Wendy bit her bottom lip. She knew after Finger Bones answered she may have to open the trapdoor for Henry. And Wendy knew if Henry ran, then Claire might follow behind him. All of the recent information definitely had *her* tummy doing giant flip-flops. But, Wendy also knew this was where she wanted to be.

Finger Bones calmly looked from Wendy, to Henry, and finally to Claire. He looked out the tree house window. He knew they deserved the truth. He looked at his hands, closing them and opening them.

"In the beginning our job was easy, almost stress-free," he said remembering the old days. "Then more and more ghosts came and it became harder to send them to their next destination. They become more stubborn and defiant ghosts. Soon reports began to emerge of these rebellious ghosts preparing the way for 'him'. Some referred to him as 'The Boss'. I don't know who 'The Boss' is, yet. But yes, I believe it's true. I believe an evil *is* lurking."

Instead of heading for the trap door and running, Henry sat still. He was too scared to move. So he listened.

"I believe he's getting bolder in his attempts to attack," Finger Bones said, looking at Wendy. "Wendy, the day at the cabin was Lefty Lennie Spinsters' second attack. He had snagged me that morning."

"The morning your arm was bleeding?" Wendy asked.

"That's right. He came back to finish me that afternoon. The night of the fire was his third attack. He got me. Now, he will come after you. You need to stop him before he becomes stronger. "

Claire looked petrified. And Henry, he froze even more.

"Wait, I will not allow this. This 'Boss', or whoever he is, he's not going to scare me," Wendy announced, sounding suddenly unflinching. "Again I say we have a job to do. Let's do this."

Chapter Thirteen

Wendy heard the sliding glass doors open behind her. She knew it was Claire. Claire always went to the front door and rang the doorbell two times. Wendy could also hear Henry pedaling his bike down the street. She turned and watched him as she climbed the wooden ladder to the tree house. He jumped the curb and flew across the lawn. "He jumps that curb in exactly the same spot every time. He probably left even more tire marks this time," she said smiling.

She looked back over her shoulder to see Claire. "Good. Claire has her backpack with her." Wendy then glanced back at Henry as he jumped from his bike. He also dangled a backpack on his shoulders. Without a word, all three scrambled through the trap door, jerked the backpacks off, and threw them in a pile on the floor in the tree house.

They sat around the old trunk. Wendy pulled the key out from her shirt. She still wore it on the string along with the whistle. With the help of Henry, Wendy inserted the key and they pushed opened the squeaky lid.

"Okay you two, we need to review the materials and supplies Finger Bones taught us about yesterday. Wendy reached over and grabbed her backpack, pulling out a purple journal. Purple was Wendy's favorite color. "I did what Finger Bones said and wrote down everything we went over yesterday afternoon. My Aunt Helen gave me this journal last year for my birthday. I had stuffed it back in one of my dresser drawers. I found it last night after Mother made me clean out my sock drawer."

All three studied and memorized each plant, herb, and tool Finger Bones discussed. Until they felt confident, they repeatedly went over how the items were used when catching ghosts and sending them to their next destination. When complete, Wendy leaned closer over the trunk. She wanted to make sure each item was in its appropriate place. As she maneuvered the salt bag, she noticed the bag was kept in a tray. Then looking closer she noticed something underneath the tray.

"Henry, go grab the flashlight over on the shelf."

"Are the batteries still good in it?" he asked.

"Yeah, I just changed them out about two weeks ago. Hurry and shine the light right down here in the corner." She pointed to a small crack in the one of the bends. "I see something. But I can't tell what it is."

"Let me take a look," Henry said.

Wendy scooted away from the trunk.

While Henry moved closer, Claire shimmied toward it too, and peered around the opened lid. "What do you see under the tray, Henry?"

"Hum, I don't know." He moved the flashlight around. I'm not sure, but I think it's a book."

Wendy jumped back towards the trunk. "Let's see if we can lift the tray out of the trunk. Come on Claire, you help too."

All three worked and maneuvered their fingers around inside the trunk, trying to grab the sides of the tray to lift from it.

While lifting, the tray shifted. "Ouch, it pinched my fingers!" Claire hollered, jerking back her hand.

"Ah. No use. We can't lift it," Henry moaned in a defeated voice. He turned to put the flashlight back on the shelf.

Wendy and Claire sat against the tree house walls looking beat. Claire continued to whine about her fingers. She had no desire to try again. Wendy, however, being the thinker of the group, was not about to let some old tray in an old trunk get the best of her. Her stubborn and determined side surfaced.

Wendy reached deep into her the pocket of her jacket and pulled out a piece of bubblegum. She threw Claire and Henry a piece. The aroma of the sweet smell filled the air as they plopped the pink juicy gum in their mouths. Wendy began to think as she chewed.

She placed both of her hands, palms down, on one side of the trunk. She closed her eyes and felt around for anything that might help her figure out how to lift the tray. She knew there had to be a lever or a button somewhere on the thing. Wendy slowly ran her fingers across the side of the rough wood and over the aged metal. On one side, she noticed the metal felt different. It was a pattern of a plain etched star. She opened her eyes to find it was golden in color. Then a shifting sound was heard. The etching of the star glowed, and the tray rose from the trunk.

"Oh wow, look, Henry!" Wendy said.

"Look at what? I know we failed," he said disappointed.

"No, we didn't. Look!"

"What?" Henry whirled around. The broadest smile covered his face from ear to ear when he saw the tray rising.

Wendy leaned in and reached for the book in the trunk. It was old and tattered and made of worn leather. Wendy looked on the front and back of the book. No writing could be found. "This has got to be Finger Bones' book," Wendy said, opening the leather cover. She carefully turned the aging pages. "It's hand written. There's a section on plants and herbs in the journal. I also see a section on levels of ghosts, on how to capture them, and on how to send them to their next destination."

"I'm guessing Toole, the old lady who hunted ghosts before Finger Bones, told him to keep a journal also. And this is it," Claire said.

"I think you're correct. Hey, here's a section in the journal labeled *Protection against Ghosts*," Wendy said. "We do need to make sure we set out all the protection items Finger Bones mentioned."

"Henry, look behind you. There's a box that has iron horseshoes in it. Dad brought five of them home to set up the game, Horseshoes. He piled them in a box and stuck it way back in the garage. He hasn't thought about them since. There are also some nails in a mason jar beside the box, and a hammer. Henry, you start hanging the horseshoes. Claire,

Mom has about three small aloe plants on the back porch. You go get them. And I will..."

"Ugh." Henry said, after opening the box of horseshoes. "What's that smell, Wendy?" He wrinkled up his nose in disgust. "I don't see any horseshoes. All I see is this gross stuff."

Claire let go of the trapdoor. She smiled and said, "I can't believe Henry T. Bartlett's grossed out by anything. I've got to see this."

"Oh, good grief Henry, it's just garlic," Wendy said. So it's got a little smell to it. If it prevents ghosts from entering the tree house we need this, gross stuff. And if you will look, you'll find the horseshoes under the garlic."

Henry quickly grabbed the horseshoes. He closed the lid and twitched his nose. He grabbed the nails and hammer, throwing them into the other box containing the horseshoes. "You can start hanging the gross garlic stuff. I'm going outside on the deck."

Wendy and Claire and Henry went to work. About twenty minutes later all protection items were placed.

"After Mom and I finished cleaning out my drawer last night, I helped her clean out a small closet in the hallway. We found this red checkered tablecloth and Mom donated it to the tree house. Wendy stood up, turned around, and walked over to the shelf. She picked up the table cloth bringing it over to the trunk. "I thought we could place this over the trunk so it would look like a table. Claire, didn't your Grandmother Pearl give you some artificial flowers last year at your piano recital?"

"She sure did."

"You said something the other day about they were in your way in your room. If you don't mind, we could use them as the centerpiece. What do you think?"

"Hey pretty good idea. That's good way to conceal the trunk."

"I can bring three old pillows," Henry said. "Tom and I share rooms. We had matching pillows on our beds. My sister, Susie, thought she had to have the same one until Mom finally put her foot down. She decided to change Susie's room to pink. Of course, Susie wouldn't consider it until I told her pink was my second favorite color in the whole wide World," Henry said with his face turning red from embarrassment. "Of course it's not! I just had to say that for her to agree to the new colors in her room. Our new colors in our room are brown and blue. You know boy colors. We were using reds."

Wendy and Claire giggled. "We can use the pillows to sit on around the table," Wendy said. "Thanks Henry. And it was good of you to convince Susie about changing her room."

Henry smiled. His face turned as red as the tablecloth.

Wendy turned her attention again to the trunk. "Now the trunk will be disguised and the tree house will be protected," Wendy said. "You two hop on your bikes and go get the flowers and pillows. Meet me back here in thirty minutes to cover the trunk," Wendy said, placing Finger Bones' journal and her own journal back in the secret compartment.

Wendy and Claire and Henry met back at the tree house. They stocked each of their backpacks with salt, hotfoot powder, and catnip. In the garage, Wendy found three soda bottles, one for each to keep in their bags. She also found some old corks and cut them to fit the tops. Finally, she picked up the three sheets of paper she had gotten from her mother's printer and some scissors from her room. She handed them to Claire. Claire cut the paper in strips and stuffed at least six in each backpack. Wendy made sure a pencil was placed in with the strips.

Wendy then grabbed Henry's backpack and unzipped one of the compartments. "Henry, why do you have balloons in here?"

"You stuff those balloons right back in there. Never know when balloons might come in handy. There are other ways for a kid to protect themselves besides plants."

"I'm sure Henry. I'm not arguing," Wendy giggled. She looked again into the bag pulling out several TV guides from one of the larger compartments.

"Put those back too."

"Henry, you still collect TV Guides?"

"Sure I do. I'm telling you, one day all of you will see. TV Guides are a useful item. I also have a slingshot along with a few rocks in there. I packed a knife my brother gave me, a red handkerchief, some string, and a baseball he didn't want anymore. I decided it wouldn't hurt to have some back-up items."

"Well alright then," Claire said, sounding as serious as Henry.

"We need wintergreen leaves. I almost forgot," Wendy said. "The leaves will help keep the mean ghosts out of our houses. We can pack a wintergreen bag to take home. Place a couple of them under your pillow. They say it's good to put them in your pocket too. If we meet Lefty Lennie Spinsters now we'll be prepared."

After all was said and done, the three gazed around the tree house proud of their accomplishment for the afternoon. They sat around for an hour or so more talking. They knew they needed to do some researching in order to find Lefty Lennie Spinsters.

To end the afternoon, Mrs. Winkelmann called out the back door, "Wendy time for dinner."

Each grabbed their items and stuffed them into the backpack to carry home for protection. They agreed to meet again during the week. The time would be decided later.

Chapter Fourteen

The long yellow school buses' engines could be heard humming outside the school as the children ran out the front doors when the three o'clock bell sounded. Wendy was on her way to the library. Every now and then she did a little hop as she walked. Every chance, she wanted to research on the notorious Lefty Lennie Spinsters. Leaving the school grounds, Wendy crossed Myrtle Street, walking briskly along the sidewalk, passing the courthouse. She picked up a stick from the dirt and rattled it against a fence as she skipped.

She shut out its clatter as she reflected on the assignment her teacher had given her just before the bell rang. Mrs. Ingram announced that by the end of the week each student should write down a title for a report. It could be about an important person, place, or thing. The only stipulation was that it had to be about Bridgeville.

When Miss Ingram finished explaining all the details of the assignment, Wendy and Claire and Henry looked at each other with interest. Wendy knew right away who she would write her report about.

The clattering sound stopped at the end of the fence row. Wendy dropped the stick, looked both ways, and crossed over to West Street where the library was located.

She bounded through the front doors of the library and scanned the room for Mrs. Taylor. Wendy called, "Hello, Mrs. Taylor, where are you?" She went behind the counter and pulled off her schoolbag chunking it under part of the counter.

"What's all that noise?" Mrs. Taylor asked in a low voice. She walked toward the checkout counter where Wendy was impatiently waiting on the inside of the counter.

Without skipping a beat and in one breath, Wendy told Mrs. Taylor all about her assignment, "…And I was +wondering if I could tell you what I thought about writing mine on. I would like to have your input because this is really important."

"Hold on Wendy, slow down child. Now, you said you had an assignment and it's to be a report."

146

"Yes ma'am," Wendy said, calming down. She took in a deep breath and let the air out gradually. "Miss Ingram said she was going to give two grades. We are to write a report for one grade. The report can be on a person of importance here, or a certain place, or a thing, like the courthouse. Then we have to make a poster about our report. We can draw it, take pictures, or write important parts about the topic on the board. For our second grade, we have to stand up in front of the classroom and tell the class about our report using the poster as our visual."

Mrs. Taylor looked at Wendy with interest. "I see. Yes, it does sound like an important assignment. So who were you thinking of writing your report on, Wendy?"

Sounding excited again, Wendy blurted, "I thought about writing my report on the notorious, Lefty Lennie Spinsters!"

Mrs. Taylor fumbled for the counter with her aged hands, dropping her book. It clattered loudly, hitting the hardwood floor, echoing through the library. The silence it left behind felt awkward. Wendy ran around from behind the counter.

"Mrs. Taylor, are you alright?" Wendy ran to get the nearest chair she could find. "Here, sit down."

"Why thank you child," Mrs. Taylor said, grabbing the edge of the chair as she sat.

Wendy hurried behind the counter, grabbed a Dixie cup and went to fill it at the water fountain. "Here, I got you some water to drink. You always said water could refresh the body and help any ailment."

"Thank you, Wendy," Mrs. Taylor said with a small smile. She accepted the cup and took a sip. "That did the trick, I feel much better already."

Wendy was still concerned though. "Are you sure? Do you want me to run and get my Dad? He'll know what to do."

"Oh no, Wendy, I'm fine." Mrs. Taylor replied, waving a hand. She closed her eyes and slowly shook her head like she was clearing it to think. She then opened them and looked at

Wendy with her gentle eyes. "It's that name. It gave me a shock when you said it. After all these years, the mere mention of his name still unnerves me." Mrs. Taylor drained the remains of her drink then slowly got to her feet, placing the Dixie cup on the counter.

As Mrs. Taylor made her way toward the microfilm room she looked over her shoulder and motioned with her fingers. "Follow me. I have some articles that could be useful to your report."

Mrs. Taylor ushered Wendy into a small, dark room. "This room contains a microfilm machine which shows miniature photographic copies of all the newspapers ever printed in Bridgeville." She carefully leaned over, switching the machine to the 'on' position. Next she turned to a shelf containing boxes of hard discs. She propped her reading glasses on the end of her nose and began flipping through them.

"Let me see, that's not it. Nope, not it either. I'm looking for a disc that will have *The Bridgeville Newspapers of*

1955 on the label. Ah, here it is," Mrs. Taylor said in a soft voice. She pulled out the hard disc, twisted it around, and inserted it into the microfilm scanner.

"See here, you skim through until you find what you want. All the newspaper clippings are saved on these discs." After a few long seconds, Mrs. Taylor continued, "If I remember correctly it should be about here. Ah yes, this is it." She tilted her head back a little more so she could better read the title through her bifocals. This particular article is titled, *Welcome to The Bridgeville Jewel Box*." She pulled out a chair and told Wendy to sit down so she could see.

Above the article, there was a picture of The Jewel Box and standing at the front doors were five people side-by-side. Wendy noticed one particular couple. They held a long ribbon in their hands. The gentlemen appeared to be about to cut with a pair of elaborate looking scissors. Pointing to the pair, Wendy asked, "Mrs. Taylor, who's this couple in the picture? The lady actually favors you in the face."

Mrs. Taylor bent to have a closer look and said tenderly, "You are looking at my sister. You call her Mrs. Harper. Her full name is Mrs. Caroline Jean Rubottom Harper. Rubottom was her maiden name. And the gentleman standing beside her was her beloved husband, Mr. Grady P. Harper. I wanted you to see the article and picture of the opening of the store.

They were newlyweds and had just bought the business. Initially, an elder couple had owned the jewelry store. They'd owned it for over twenty years. After a robbery, they closed the doors and placed a for sale sign on the door."

Wendy raised her eyebrows. She had never realized Mrs. Harper had once been married. She studied the picture some more. She could tell by the expression on their faces they were happy. But she wondered what this article had to do with Lefty Lennie Spinsters.

Without saying a word, Mrs. Taylor leaned across Wendy and scanned the newspaper clippings for a second time. She stopped when she came to one which read, *Tragedy at The*

Bridgeville Jewel Box. "The story was written and printed the very afternoon after the robbery," she said somberly. "The Jewelry Box was one of many places Lefty Lennie Spinsters robbed during his crime spree. Caroline's husband was shot and killed. When Lefty Lennie started shooting, Grady jumped in front of Caroline, saving her life. Before the police arrived, Lefty Lennie Spinsters escaped in his car, more or less empty handed."

Mrs. Taylor turned away from Wendy and walked a couple of steps and stopped, "Caroline and I discussed that horrible afternoon many years later. She recalled she had been in the vault room in the back of the store. Jewelry and money were kept in the vault. Caroline was taking inventory.

On one wall in the back were some built-in cabinets with a sink, a refrigerator, and a small wooden table with chairs. Caroline had decided to take a break and was pouring a coffee when she heard the noise of a car's engine and the screeching of tires. Shortly after, she told she heard an almighty bang and the sounds of breaking glass. It was such a shock she was frozen to the spot with a coffee cup and pot still in her hands.

Mrs. Taylor paused once more. She turned back toward Wendy and said, "Then Caroline said she heard this horrible gruff voice coming from the front of the store. It kept repeating the same thing, over and over, 'Where's the watch? Give me the watch and nobody gets hurt.' Terrified by what she was hearing, Caroline hollered out for Grady. She ran toward the curtain separating the back from the front.

And that's when it happened," Mrs. Taylor whispered as her head dropped. After a moment, she composed herself. Lifted her head back up and looked at Wendy. "You see, Lefty Lennie Spinsters had crashed through the window of the store in his car. He had a loaded machine gun pointed at Grady and was demanding the watch. It was at that point Caroline ran screaming toward the curtains. Lefty Lennie took aim at her and seeing what was about to happen Grady jumped in front and took the bullets. Both went plummeting to the ground taking the curtains and rod down with them."

Mrs. Taylor took a shallow breath. "Lefty Lennie ransacked a few more display cases bashing them with his gun. In the end, he never found the watch he was after and drove away with only a few minor jewelry pieces. He left with Grady dying in Caroline's arms."

Wendy sat stunned. She felt terrible she had chosen Lefty Lennie Spinsters for her report and causing fresh agony to Mrs. Taylor. "Mrs. Taylor, I'm so sorry. I can choose another topic. I didn't mean..."

"Wendy," interrupted Mrs. Taylor, "the incident happened over fifty years ago. Despite what happened, sister's still managed to live a happy and satisfying life. This is an excellent topic to write on for your class report. I know my sister would also agree. I just want you to understand the kind of person Lefty Lennie Spinsters really was. Okay?"

"Okay," Wendy said quietly. Mrs. Taylor had no idea how much Wendy *did* understand about Lefty Lennie Spinsters.

"Now, turn around and let me show you one final story which was printed only three days after his capture. There are not many books on the cart this afternoon, so while you're reading I'm going to put them back on the shelf." She stopped turning the microfilm knob. "Ah, here it is. This newspaper article made the front page that day. It is titled, *The Notorious Life and Capture of Lefty Lennie Spinsters*. It's rather long. The person who wrote this spent many hours interviewing people. She even interviewed Lefty Lennie. By the time you finish it will be almost time to close."

"Yes ma'am. And Mrs. Taylor, thank you."

"Why, you are very welcome, Wendy."

Wendy turned slowly in the chair and began reading the front of the 1955 newspaper article. The entire front page was dedicated to the story. It began by telling of a respected couple of Bridgeville, Mr. and Mrs. Allen Spinsters.

'They had one son. His name was Lennie Spinsters. He had lived his childhood being *raised as an only child with his mother and father. He was called by the name*

155

Lennie through his childhood years. His parents owned a small farm three miles south of Bridgeville in a small community called Basin.

In a recent interview with Lennie's parents, Lennie seemed to be a normal acting child. He played, went to school, and worked chores at home like other kids. Then around eleven or twelve years of age, Lennie began acting different. He started running around with some older boys. He stole items and pocketed from the locals in Bridgeville. He seemed to grow distant from family, and friends at school. He stopped staying around the house. By age fifteen Lennie had been in so much trouble, he developed a nickname, Lefty.

One day, the group of boys were annoying and terrorizing the downtown streets of Bridgeville. During the attack, Lennie decided to deliberately knock down an elder gentleman. What Lennie did not realize, until it was too late, was the strength of the man. Lennie's intentions were to steal the man's wallet. Instead, the older man pulled Lennie down to the sidewalk with him.

After a moment of struggling, Lennie emerged standing with a small gun in his grips which materialized from the gentleman's pockets.

The terrified man threw his arms in the air begging for his life. And if Lennie had told the truth, the incident scared him too. It scared him so bad his left eye began switching. But Lennie gave a phony laugh demanding his money. Afterwards, the story grew and grew. Soon Lennie Spinsters became the notorious, Lefty Lennie Spinsters.

The article went on to read about how several years later, Lefty Lennie left the small time crooks and commenced to robbing trains, stores, and banks. Everyone within a hundred mile radius knew of Lefty Lennie Spinsters or had some type of occurrence with him. He was definitely a feared man.

Three days after the incident, Lefty Lennie Spinsters was branded a murderer. Right in the very town he had been raised, Lefty Lennie killed Mr. Grady P. Harper, husband of Caroline Jean Harper and owner of The Bridgeville Jewel Box.

After an interview with the widow, the shaken Mrs. Harper said she had been in the back storage room when Lefty Lennie Spinsters rammed his motor vehicle through the front glass of the store. Bewildered by such a clatter of noise, Mrs. Harper said she called out to her husband. As she approached the entranceway to the front she could hear a brusque male voice roar, "Where's the watch? Give me the watch and nobody gets hurt."

She reported she then heard a round of firing followed by something slamming into her, knocking her to the store's floor. To her horror, the impact was her husband's body collapsing against her from the forceful impact of the bullets. Mrs. Harper's husband died a few moments later.

After a failed attempt to rob the jewelry store of a supposedly rare watch, Lefty jumped back into the car. For a brief moment, Mrs. Harper stated he made eye contact with her before he left. Staring straight into his eyes she could see each nervous twitch his left eye made. He then growled angrily out loud, backed out slamming into another parked car, and tore off down the street firing warning shots into the air.

A posse of law enforcement as well as citizens quickly formed, searching for Lefty Lennie Spinsters late into the night and into the next day. By the time the sun evaporated the dew off the ground, a hundred thousand dollar bounty was set for the live capture of Lefty Lenny Spinsters. Some townspeople in the search were sent to cover entranceways leading into and out of Bridgeville. Others rushed door-to-door searching through each and every store, house, and barn located in the town. No rock went unturned.

After three long days of intensive searching, a smaller more experienced group of law enforcement tracked and finally captured Lefty Lennie on the southeast side of Bridgeville. He was found shockingly clawing the sides of the bank of Bone River. His fingers bled from hours of desperately digging at the hard clay sides filled with small stones and roots. One police officer claimed they wouldn't have found him if it weren't for hearing his frantic moans and cries. And due to low waters, a narrow trail was discovered which traveled down the side of the bank to a hard clay and stone platform.

Lefty Lennie Spinsters was captured on the bank of Bone River. He staggered and acted irrational and scared. His eyes were large and wild. He repeated over and while being handcuffed, "It's his fault, not mine. Can't you hear him? You do not have much time. He's evil! He made me do it. He *made me shoot. He made me do it all. Look at him. He's laughing. It's his fault, not mine.*

Wendy paused a moment. She then flipped the screen to the next article. It was published some years later. Wendy turned around in her chair to see if she saw Mrs. Taylor. She turned back to the screen and read the next article.

Lefty Lennie Spinsters Dies in Jail

Lefty Lennie spent many years alone in the Bridgeville's jail. He saw daylight for only thirty minutes every twenty-four hours. They say the loneliness and dreariness of the cell can drive the strongest man insane. The officer on duty the day Lefty Lennie died said Lefty Lennie had just finished eating his lunch and had lain down for a nap. Suddenly, from a deep sleep,

Lefty Lennie Spinsters sat straight up and began yelling, "No, no, you said you would not kill me. I did everything you asked Boss. Leave me alone. Help me, somebody help..." He clutched his throat, jerked back against the cell walls and fell over dead.

Wendy flipped back to the previous article. She reread where Lefty Lennie had cried out in terror. *'Can't you hear him? You do not have much time. He's evil! He made me do it.'* Then she flipped to the last article where Lefty Lenny hollered out, *'I did everything you asked Boss.'*

Wendy Dee Winkelmann turned off the microfilm scanner, pushed her chair back, and she sat staring at the blank screen. "Who was Lefty Lennie hollering at and what did 'The Boss' make him do?" she whispered.

Wendy silently thought while looking out of the small room. *I wonder what it was like being one of the many hunting for Lefty Lennie Spinsters. And Mrs. Harper, she had to be scared and tormented sitting and waiting at her home.*

Wendy went to find Mrs. Taylor. She glanced up at the large round clock hanging on the wall. "Fifteen minutes till five? Wow, I read for an hour and fifteen minutes? That has to be a record."

Wendy searched the library for Mrs. Taylor. "Where is she? She told me she didn't have many books to place back on the shelves today." Walking past the counter, Wendy eyed a piece of paper containing a list of about forty to fifty books. "Oh no, these are all the books she had to put up today." Wendy felt guilty. "Mrs. Taylor, Mrs. Taylor, where are you?"

"Woo-hoo, I'm over here, Wendy." Mrs. Taylor peeked from around a bookshelf. "That was the last book. I'm finished. Now, did you read the article?"

"Yes ma'am I did and I'm so sorry you had so many books to put up. I should have helped first."

"Nonsense," Mrs. Taylor said, waving her hand at Wendy. She pushed the cart up to the counter. "Determining your topic for your report was most important. Now, I have one thing to show you before we lock up for the day." Mrs.

Taylor sauntered over to the counter and around to the inside. She leaned over reaching for something. Wendy saw Mrs. Taylor had a huge scrapbook. She placed the scrapbook on the counter.

"What a *huge* scrapbook, Mrs. Taylor," Wendy said with raised eyebrows.

Flipping casually through the pages, she said, "Yes it is, Wendy. In this scrapbook, I have saved every newspaper article I've come across on Lefty Lennie Spinsters. The newspaper articles include anything from petty theft to the murder of my brother-in-law."

"Oh, wow, there were a lot of stories written on him."

"And on almost every anniversary another story is published. Why, here's the article written just last year on Lefty Lennie Spinsters," Mrs. Taylor said, tapping the story taped to the page.

Wendy glanced at the article. Last year's article pertained more to the success of The Bridgeville Jewelry Box and how the store itself had remained family owned. There were two pictures printed for the article. The first was the picture for the opening of the store fifty-seven years ago. The second picture was taken last year. Mrs. Caroline Jean Harper stood happily in front of the store in both pictures.

"Here Wendy, I want you to take this scrapbook to help write your report." She smiled as she handed it to her.

Wendy returned the smile. "I'll take care of the scrapbook, Mrs. Taylor."

"I do not have any doubt," Mrs. Taylor said tenderly, patting Wendy's hand.

Chapter Fifteen

After handing the scrapbook to Wendy, Mrs. Taylor decided to lighten the mood. "Wendy put the scrapbook in your book bag. I'm going to close the library five minutes early today. I have to go to The Bridgeville Jewelry Box for Sister."

"What for?" Wendy asked, carefully placing the scrapbook with her school books.

"I found an old pocket watch in our safe at the Rubottom Plantation. For years, the watch sat in the safe at The Bridgeville Jewel Box. The watch I'm referring to was bought by Mrs. Lorna Grapples when the first owners ran it. I guess Sister decided she would keep it at home since both parties were now deceased."

"What kind of watch is it?"

"It is an antique pocket watch which was created and made for Abner Grapples. Other than that, I don't know. I had forgotten she had the watch. It was purchased seventy-five years ago from The Bridgeville Jewel Box. I took the watch out and wound it up, but it wouldn't run. So I placed the watch in my purse this morning. I'm going to surprise Sister by having the watch cleaned and repaired."

Wendy knew Mrs. Taylor and Mrs. Harper lived at Rubottom Plantation. They were raised there as children. The two sisters were the only ones who lived there now.

"Neat, she'll be pleased. She can enjoy the watch again after all this time," Wendy said, zipping her book bag and throwing it over her shoulders.

"Well, she never wore or used the watch. This pocket watch has historical value. It was initially purchased by a Mrs. Lorna Grapples in 1937. Mrs. Lorna had the watch especially made for her husband's birthday."

"Abner Grapples, the one who is buried at the old cemetery on Screaming Hollow Road?"

"Yes, he's the one," Mrs. Taylor answered. "Mrs. Lorna gave him the watch at his birthday party almost one year prior to the day she died."

Mrs. Taylor turned and picked up two CD's, placing them in their appropriate cases. Wendy then took them and quickly placed them on a nearby shelf. "Okay, the CD's are back on the shelf. You can continue."

"Thank you, Wendy. Let me see, I was speaking about the party. Yes, well, when Mrs. Lorna presented him with the watch, Grapples laughed in her face. He claimed the watch was a disgraceful gift. Especially after all he had given her. He had given her a name, and the name made her somebody of importance. He spoke with disdain telling her the clothes she wore were sewn from the finest materials and that she should be ashamed repaying him with such a gift.

The majority of the guests who attended the party knew different though. Abner Grapples had turned into a cruel husband over the years. He became a miserly angry man. His appearance and facial features even turned ugly. He forbade Mrs. Lorna to have friends or attend any kind of social events outside the home. And her taking a job was out of the question."

"How terrible, why didn't she just leave old Grapples?"

"She felt she had nowhere else to go I suppose. She had no family she knew of. Mrs. Lorna Grapples was an orphaned baby. A city employee at the time found her in a box behind the library when she was a baby."

"Why did he marry her?"

"Abner Grapples wanted the best of everything and she was the most beautiful lady around. He courted her and won her affection with his youthful charm. But he didn't love her."

168

"I don't like old man Grapples and I've never met him."

"Not many people liked him who knew him," Mrs. Taylor chuckled. "Oh, to begin with the townspeople did. Grapples moved here as a young lad. Girls swooned over the young Abner. He was handsome and charming.

He proved to be a hard worker as soon as he came here too. Not a lazy bone in his body. He wanted the best of everything, but he wanted it for himself. It didn't take young Abner long to decide working for others wasn't for him. He soon ventured out on his own and started his own business.

He bought a ferry boat and made his first bundle of money. The ferry boat transported people and supplies across Bone River in and out of Bridgeville. The business thrived until the bridge was built. This didn't deter Abner Grapples though. He turned his attention to the railroad and bought stock."

"I heard he hoarded all the money he made and still died a lonely man. He thought he had it all. Seems to me he had nothing," Wendy said with a nod.

"You are correct, Wendy," Mrs. Taylor said.

"Mrs. Taylor, what happened after the birthday party?" Wendy asked.

Mrs. Taylor waved her hand in the air. "Oh yes, I was talking about the birthday party. Well those attending the party left, ashamed of how Abner Grapples talked to his wife. And Mrs. Lorna went to bed, broken hearted, and alone." She paused for a moment clicking the mouse on her computer to shut it down.

"He was cruel," Wendy said with narrowed eyes.

"He was. But let me tell you, Mrs. Lorna woke the next morning and dressed as she always had for her husband. She cooked his breakfast and cleaned the house. After he left for work, she then returned to The Bridgeville Jewel Box with the watch. No one would have believed what had taken place at the party the night before by the way Mrs. Lorna behaved. She seemed as happy and content as she always did."

When the computer turned off, Mrs. Taylor picked up a stapler and began stapling a stack of papers while she talked. "One other couple had owned the store prior to Sister and her husband. The watch had been bought during that time. Then when Sister and her husband bought the store, they were told about the watch and asked to store it in the safe. It was placed in the same fancy box it had been stored in for years."

"Why did she have the watch stored at the store?"

As far as I know, Mrs. Lorna never told the owners *why* she had the pocket watch put in the safe at the store or why she had it engraved. Sister honored their wishes for Mrs. Lorna. Sister and I always believed Mrs. Lorna had hoped Grapples would change his mind, and his heart. But he never did. No one ever knew Mrs. Lorna had the watch engraved except the previous owners, Sister, me, and now of course you."

"Oh, if old man Grapples were here today, I would tell him a thing or two."

Mrs. Taylor finished stapling, stacked the papers neatly, and placed them in a folder. After sliding the folder into a drawer, she reached under the counter and picked up her purse. She took out a box and removed the pocket watch. "When I found the watch, I opened the face of it and read where Mrs. Lorna had a poem engraved on the inside cover. The writing circles the outer edge and winds around to the center."

"Oh great, there's more and it gets sadder? I feel so bad for Mrs. Grapples."

Mrs. Taylor patted Wendy on the shoulder. "I believe the poem will confuse you more instead of making you gloomier. At least it did me."

Wendy looked at Mrs. Taylor with interest.

Mrs. Taylor propped her glasses on her nose. She held the watch and turned it so she could read the engraved words.

"The Winds of Time I call to unlock,
the past a passage which has been blocked.
A name and place enclosed you will find.
bring past to present I plead you to bind."

"What does it mean?" Wendy asked.

Mrs. Taylor looked closer at the watch. "I haven't figured it out. The watch has a secret compartment behind the engraving. See this latch? See if you can open it."

Wendy carefully took the watch and grabbed the latch. She pulled it open to find a tiny empty compartment. She had this strange feeling in her gut. *This can't be the watch Lefty Lennie hunted. There's no way. This is just a unique, strange...oh my, this very well could be the watch Lefty Lennie has been hunting for!* Wendy gazed at it and after a second or so, she shrugged her shoulders. *What am I thinking? Oh good grief, it's just a watch.* Wendy closed the lids, and handed the watch back to Mrs. Taylor. She didn't give it another thought.

Mrs. Taylor placed the watch back in the box. "Okay, let's get moving," Mrs. Taylor said, picking up her purse. "Go around and make sure the lights are turned out." Mrs. Taylor walked toward the front door. "We'll leave this light on so the police officer can see inside when he drives by for his nightly check."

Wendy scuttled around the library turning off lights. "Okay, I have all the lights turned off, except this one in the front," Wendy said, walking out the door behind Mrs. Taylor.

"Are you walking home today, Wendy?" Mrs. Taylor asked, locking the front door.

"Yes ma'am I am."

"I will be more than happy to drive you home if you want. I just need to drop off the watch," she said, checking the doors one last time.

"Thank you, but I'm fine."

"Well okay. I will see you soon." Before Wendy walked away Mrs. Taylor called her name. "Wendy."

"Yes, Mrs. Taylor."

"Please be careful."

"Yes ma'am. I sure will." Wendy said, looking into Mrs. Taylor's eyes as she walked away. Wendy was almost positive she saw worry in her eyes.

Chapter Sixteen

Wendy took the levee when walking home from the library. It wrapped all the way around Bridgeville. It was built in the early 1900's to protect the town from the rivers. At the top of it, a sidewalk was built. Wendy climbed up the cement stairs behind the library and began skipping towards home.

A train trestle and the railroad tracks were located half way between town and home. So when Wendy reached the train trestle, she climbed down the steps and played on the tracks for a while. She knew she wasn't supposed to stop anywhere on her way home, but she wasn't going to stay very long. What harm could it cause? She played on the tracks many times before.

Wendy approached the railroad tracks. She looked to her left and then to her right. "Nope, no train." The last train ran at four o'clock each afternoon and had for years. Wendy stepped over the train railings. She stood in the middle of the tracks facing the trestle and skipped. When she reached the train trestle, she stopped and turned in the opposite direction on the tracks.

Hopping and playing again, she jumped from one foot to the other on the crossties. As she made one leap, she felt a vibration under her feet, so she stopped. She looked up and froze. Her heart seemed to stop in her chest. In front of her was a huge round blaring light, barreling toward her. She immediately knew it was a train and she needed to move, and fast. But there was no time. Wendy quickly raised her arms for protection. Knowing the effort was futile, she squatted for the impact. But surprisingly, no impact happened and to her disbelief she was still alive.

Wendy slowly stood. She had the strangest feeling. As she lowered her arms and opened her eyes, one at a time, she couldn't believe what she saw. A bluish ghostly train was racing down the tracks and running directly through her. *Wham and whoosh!* She felt the force of the wind slamming into her body. It flapped her clothes and blew her hair wildly as it flew by.

The roaring sound of the train whistle and the clickety-clack of the wheels churning on the tracks vibrated in her ears. Gazing up, Wendy saw black smoke pulsing through the air coming from the steam locomotive. Her head felt dizzy. Objects within the compartments of the train were whizzing by at such speeds her balance became unstable.

Finally, the caboose zoomed by whirling Wendy around. The force threw back her head as if something had been pulled from her body. Still feeling woozy, Wendy gazed down the tracks. The ghost train raced away into the night.

Wendy took a step, teetered, and then was able to right herself by throwing her arms out to the side. When she gained her balance, she then stood straight up. She took in a deep breath and slowly let it out as she lowered her arms.

At that moment, Wendy heard someone screaming. The sound came from the river waters.

"Help me! Somebody help me please!"

Still feeling somewhat dazed, Wendy scrambled over to the trestle. Without much success, she called, "H-h-hello." She cleared her throat, cupped her hands, and yelled again. "Hello, is anyone down there? Do you need help?" She waited and listened. "Hello?" She peeked over the side of the trestle. She could hear the sounds of the water below whooshing and whirling around rocks and rushing downstream. But, she heard no reply.

Wendy felt a knot in her stomach. What if someone was really hurt and couldn't respond? "Hello, are you hurt? If you're down there and you can't speak try to throw something." Out of the blue, a voice beside her answered proudly, "I'm right here and I'm just fine. I'm not hurt one bit."

"What?" Wendy whirled around.

A boy who looked to be about thirteen dusted off his clothes and repeated with a broad smile, "I said I'm fine and I'm not hurt one bit."

A puzzled looked washed over Wendy. She pointed down to the river. Then she narrowed her eyes, glaring at the boy. "This is *not* the time to be funny. Someone was hollering for help. You could at least help me instead of making fun of me."

The boy leaned back and raised his eyebrows.

Wendy turned back toward the train trestle. "Hey, I'm going to get help!"

"Okay, but I'm telling you, I'm fine," the boy said, raising his eyebrows and nodding his head.

Wendy turned to face the boy again. The glare of the sun prevented her from seeing him clearly. So she took a step back and shifted to the side. Her eyes then grew wide. "Hey, you...you are..."

"Willie Porter is my name. And your name is?"

"I am Wendy, Wendy Dee Winkelmann," she answered, stunned and staring at Willie.

"Nice to meet you, Wendy," Willie said, clasping his thumbs in his overalls straps, rocking back and forth on his heels.

"Uh-huh." Wendy said, continuing to gape.

Willie gave a small chuckle. "Are you okay, Wendy? You look like you have seen a ghost!"

Wendy nodded her head in agreement.

"Ah, I'm just messing with you," Willie said, waving his hand. "Yes, I *am* a ghost." He looked down at himself and then back at Wendy. "Well, what do you think?"

"I think I can see right through you. And you're glowing," she said, still a little dumbfounded. But to me, I think you look fine for a ghost." She didn't tell him his overalls were rather short and his shirt could use some sewing. She knew Mrs. Wilkins, the town's seamstress, could mend his shirt in no time.

Then she thought about the person in distress. "Oh no, I forgot about the person screaming for help!" Wendy cried.

Willie threw up his hands, "Oh it's okay. Really, I can explain."

"Explain what?"

"The cry for help...was me."

"What? Are you kidding?"

"No, I'm not kidding at all."

"I'm getting more confused by the minute," Wendy said, shaking her head.

"Please, let me explain. You see, I fell off this very bridge years and years ago. It happened one afternoon as I was walking home from school. I was *never* supposed to walk over the train trestle, but on this particular day I was so excited I thought one day taking the short cut wouldn't matter.

I had gotten an A on my math test and I wanted to hurry home to show my pops. You see, he was a stickler for good grades. My older brother, Sam, he always got good grades. But me, I had to work hard to get this A. I had been coming home with C's and D's. So you see I had to get home early. I knew Sam would bring home his good grades and I wanted Pops to see mine first, so I'd make him proud."

"What happened on the train trestle, Willie? How did you fall off?" Wendy asked, listening closely.

"I had never known the train to be early. My luck, the train was that day. It came barreling over before I could reach the other side. I fell over. Not being able to swim, I drowned.

And now I go through the motions of the train roaring over the trestle and me drowning over and over every day."

"I'm so sorry. Did you find out why the train was early?"

"Oh, I heard two men had escaped from the jail the night before. They hid out down by the river overnight and into the next day. They hijacked the train when it was preparing its last run for the day."

She stayed quiet about the matter and asked, "Is it awful? I mean, drowning every day?"

"In the beginning it was pre-tty bad. I didn't understand what was happening and didn't realize I was a ghost. As the years dragged by, I realized what was going on, and falling off the trestle and drowning in the river got less and less painful. You know that's what ghosts do...right?"

"What drown every day?"

Willie laughed. He shook his head. "No, see when a person experiences some sort of shock or trauma during an unexpected, well you know, death, they can't see beyond those last moments before they turn into a ghost. They relive those final moments over and over."

"Oh how terrible," Wendy said shocked.

"Like I said, in the beginning it was terrible. But, because I was a good person when I was alive, and I was just at the wrong place at the wrong time, over the years the pain has been taken away."

"Well, why haven't you gone on to the next place? You know, to your next destination?"

Willie smiled. "Even before his cabin burned, Finger Bones told me I was here to do some great things before I go on to my next place. So for now I'm content."

Wendy suddenly thought about the time. "Oh no, I know it must be getting late. I need to be on my way."

"You have to leave so soon? Can you return?" Willie asked, looking disappointed.

"Oh sure, I'll come back in a couple of days. I'm walking home on Thursday too. I'll bring my two friends."

"Good, I'll be looking forward to your visit. I don't get many visitors and you're much nicer than the creepy ghost in the pajamas the other day."

Wendy started to say goodbye until she heard the words *'creepy ghost in the pajamas'*. Wendy felt a cold chill crawl up her spine. "Um, this guy you saw, what color were his pajamas? Do you remember?"

"Let me think. He was covered in mud and had dirty moss hanging all over him. So it was kind of hard to tell," Willie answered, tapping his finger on his chin. "Hum, I do believe his pajamas were black and white striped." He began nodding his head. "Yep, I'm sure of it and there were these numbers on the chest of his shirt too. Don't remember the exact numbers though. And, you know, he looked very familiar."

Wendy's eyes grew wide. She took a couple of steps towards Willie. "Willie, think hard. Did this ghost say anything about where he came from or where he was going?"

Willie looked back at Wendy. He could tell she was concerned about the matter. He also knew this ghost who had emerged from the river was a wrathful man, and he was *not* one to be taken lightly. And the spook appearing on the day Finger Bones cabin burned was definitely not a good sign.

"I tried to speak to him while he trudged passed me. He walked on a fog that floated just above the ground as he came out of the river. All he said was, 'I was sent to make ready for *The Boss*.' Then that ghost spat at the ground, looked at me with those creepy red eyes, and said, 'The Boss would win the town over this time whether they wanted him or not'."

Wendy sucked in a sharp breath and looked out over the river. She mumbled to herself, "The Boss, the one who is evil." She looked at Willie with worried eyes. She asked, "Did he say where he was headed?"

Willie looked at her. His eyebrows scrunched together as he thought. "He said he was going to where it all ended."

"He's going to where it all ended? What does that mean?" Wendy asked herself under her breath.

Chapter Seventeen

Wendy stormed in the house. She swung her jacket over a kitchen chair and threw her book bag to the floor. She ran through the house looking for her mom. She yelled out, but there was no answer. Looking out the back door, Wendy saw her mom raking leaves. "YES!" she said pleased. She rushed to the phone making a three way call to Claire and Henry.

"I've had the most interesting day of my life," Wendy said hastily. "I have so much information to tell you both. I don't want to tell you on the phone though. I've heard ghosts can hear through phones. I'm afraid the Internet or Skype won't be smart either. Can you both meet me at school early in the morning? We can talk by the tree on the playground. If I don't have time to tell you everything in the morning, I can finish at P.E. time."

Wendy met Claire and Henry on the playground at seven-fifteen in the morning. The bell rang at seven forty-five, so they had thirty minutes to talk.

When she hung up the phone, she grabbed her book bag from the floor and quickly darted to her room. Sitting on the bed, Wendy pulled the scrapbook from her book bag. She ran her hand over the cover. She felt sad for Mrs. Harper and for stirring bad memories for Mrs. Taylor. She whispered, "I promise to do my best on this report Mrs. Harper and Mrs. Taylor. And Mr. Harper, I will make sure you're the hero of the story...not Lefty Lennie Spinsters."

The next morning, all three scampered to one of the big pecan trees located on the playground. Claire and Henry were five minutes early. The moment Mrs. Winkelmann pulled up at the curb of the school the two were jumping up and down. They waved their arms at Wendy.

Wanting her friends to hear everything, Wendy started at the beginning. "I ran into the library excited about my topic.

I wanted her opinion about my topic for the report. I thought she would think it was cool what I was writing about. So when she asked me, I blurted out Lefty Lennie Spinster's name. Boy was I shocked. Mrs. Taylor almost fainted when she heard his name."

"What?" Henry asked.

"That's terrible. Why would his name have that effect on her?" Claire asked upset.

Wendy tried to give all the details of what Mrs. Taylor had said about her sister and her sister's late husband. Wendy told about the scrapbook. Claire and Henry were quiet and listened intently to Wendy. Unfortunately, soon their thirty minutes were over and the bell rang for school.

"Oh, rats. Now we have to wait until P.E.," Claire whined.

"I know. And if this gets any better, I'm going to have to bring popcorn," Henry said.

When time for P.E. the three friends scurried back to the large pecan tree farthest from the kids on the playground. Wendy, Claire, and Henry sat on one of the huge exposed roots sticking out of the ground.

"I don't know about this," Claire said fretfully.

"Oh for goodness sakes Claire, he's a ghost. I've already told you nobody can see him but us," Wendy spat aggravated. "And we can't even hear the whistle Finger Bones gave me. So what's the problem? He needs to know."

Claire picked up a small stick and scribbled in the sand. "Well, you're going to look mighty dumb standing here blowing a whistle with no sound. Our classmates are going to think you have lost your marbles."

While the girls were squabbling about calling Finger Bones, Henry glanced over at the kickball game in progress. Suddenly, he saw the funniest sight. "Oh man, Wendy and

Claire stop your jabbering or fussing or whatever you two are doing and take a look at what I see. Never mind about blowing the whistle. Look over there."

Both girls followed where he pointing. A group of kids were playing a game of kickball. Wendy and Claire's eyes grew wide. It was Finger Bones standing beside home plate. He looked over at Wendy, winked, and tipped his hat. He then bent and looked from the pitcher to Buck.

It was time for Buck Fergus to kick. The boy pitching was tall and slender. He looked extremely nervous. Standing with the kickball in both hands against his chest, he held the ball and pushed up his glasses with his thumbs.

"Roll the ball you dimwit," Buck hollered impatiently.

Every kid in the outfield bent their knees and placed their hands in ready position. Each boy and girl hoped the ball went anywhere but in their direction. Buck always kicked the high flies and he kicked them straight into the outfield. Straws were drawn before every game. The unlucky souls who drew the shortest sticks were stuck in the outfield positions. No one wanted to catch the high flying ball Buck kicked. The ones who dared ended up upside down in the garbage can, with a wedgie, or worse by the end of the school day.

Wendy and Claire and Henry stood and watched from the sheltered pecan tree. Each wondered what their new ghost friend was about to do. The pitcher swung the ball backwards down by his right side. He then came forward releasing the kickball with a strong push. Buck took one step forward with his left foot as the ball neared the plate. He was ready to nail the kickball with his right. Buck's right foot started moving forward as the ball approached the base.

At that moment in time, Finger Bones touched the tip of his nose. Sparkles of light went flying all around the home plate. Instead of the ball rolling straight across home plate, the ball changed direction and whirled around the plate. Not noticing what had happened, Buck continued forward with his kick, missed the ball, and lost his balance. His legs flew high into the air. Buck went down hitting the ground with a loud thud. Buck was making so much commotion almost the entire fourth grade was standing and watching.

"Oh my word, how much better can today get? To see Buck Fergus flying through the air and hitting the ground like a roped cow is priceless," Henry said, grabbing his stomach. He laughed so hard his stomach hurt.

Wendy and Claire were snickering too. The roar of the playground grew louder and louder until Coach Parker hurried over blowing his whistle. He discovered Buck rolling on the ground moaning and groaning. He again blew the whistle telling everyone around to stop the nonsense and go on about their business.

Finger Bones popped up smiling his broad smile next to Wendy. "Well, I think Buck will act better for a couple of days."

"I don't know. Look."

Wendy spotted the new kid in fourth grade attempting to help Buck. The boy tried to knock the dirt from Buck's pants and help him up from the ground. Instead of accepting the help, Buck shoved the boy as hard as he could and yelled, "Get your grubby hands off me you scumbag. Nobody touches me. I *sure* don't need your help."

"I think it'll take much more than getting a little embarrassed to change Buck Fergus," Wendy said, shaking her head and rolling her eyes.

"Buck is a dumwad," Claire said.

Finger Bones changed the subject. "Now, what can I help you with today?" he asked.

Wendy and Claire and Henry each found a huge root to plop down on. The roots bulged from the ground located around the tree.

"What I need to tell you Finger Bones, I haven't had time to tell Claire and Henry all of it," Wendy said.

"Well, I have plenty of time. I'm listening."

"Start talking already," Henry complained. "We've been waiting for the rest of the story for three hours. I thought I'd never make it through math."

"I know. We had to estimate sums in math problems today. I almost missed one. All I could think about was how Mr. Harper jumped and took that bullet for his wife," Claire said with a sad face.

Wendy told Finger Bones everything she had conveyed to Claire and Henry. Then she began her story of how she experienced the ghost train. She described the agonizing moments as the train droned toward her and then whizzed through her body and how she met Willie Porter at the train trestle.

Wendy then quickly got to the point. "There was this other ghost Willie saw. He said he came straight up out of the river draped in wet moss and he wore a black and white striped outfit. By the description he gave me, I was pretty sure it was Lefty Lennie Spinsters. Then when Willie told me what that ghost said, I knew the ghost was Lefty Lennie Spinsters. He told Willie he was sent to prepare for, 'The Boss'"

Standing in the shadow of the tree, Finger Bones continued to stare ahead. Wendy couldn't tell if he had heard a single word she had uttered.

"Finger Bones, did you hear what I said?"

"Oh...yes, I heard." He took in a deep breath and blinked slowly. He shifted the stick on his shoulder. "Lefty Lennie needs his energy. He' going return to the very spot where he died to reclaim the energy left behind."

"I don't understand," Claire said, chewing the inside of her bottom lip.

"All ghosts go back to the exact location where they took their last breath," Finger Bones said, propping his foot up on one of the large roots. They need the energy to acquire stamina just like you need food and water. They need their strength before they can carry out whatever purpose they have here on earth."

Finger Bones looked at Wendy. "When a person dies their energy seeps into the surrounding objects, some energy drifts in circles through the air staying close to its last place of memory."

"Whoa! Well, it has been several days since Willie Porter saw the ghost," Wendy said. "I read an article where Lefty Lennie died in his cell. That's what Lefty Lennie meant when he said he was, 'going back to where it ended', isn't it? He was meaning where his life ended. I've heard the townsfolk say many times Lefty Lennie Spinsters died a delirious man in that cell."

"He did indeed, Wendy. He did indeed," Finger Bones agreed, nodding his head.

Though keeping his voice down, Henry threw his hands up in the air. "Delirious? The man went bonkers! He was always talking to himself. Sometimes he talked to someone in his cell when no one else was there. And the day he kicked the bucket, he was screaming and hollering as though someone was literally killing him. My grandpa was just a teenager at the time and he remembers the story. He recalls people claiming Lefty Lennie went from being a tough acting man to a petrified acting youngster while living in that cell day after day."

Claire looked around the playground. She leaned in close to Wendy and Henry. She was paranoid someone might hear her, so she cupped her hands around her mouth. "My grandmother told me Lefty Lennie Spinsters was so scared about something that his heart just quit."

Henry picked up the stick Claire had. He started drawing the outline of a ghost in the dirt. "Maybe Lefty

200

Lennie was scared because there was a ghost in his cell. Maybe nobody could see the ghost but him. And maybe the ghost was, 'The Boss'."

Wendy's eyebrows immediately went up and her mouth flew open. Wendy was the thinker of the group…not Henry. She knew Henry didn't realize his idea was an excellent thought. Wendy jumped from where she sat and grabbed Henry by the shoulders. "I think you've got something Henry. What a great idea!"

"I had a great idea?" Henry repeated.

"Yes you did Henry! And I like the way you think!"

Wendy released Henry and twisted around to face Finger Bones. "The day Lefty Lennie was captured on the river banks, he acted strange, right? And by the time the police officers reached him, his fingertips were split open from clawing the dirt," she said, rubbing her thumb over her four fingers on both hands. "He repeated over and over that all the crimes were someone else's fault. He even cried out at one point, 'Look at him. He is laughing. It's not my fault. He made me do it'." I believe he was talking to someone no one could see."

Claire jumped from where she sat. "Wendy, pipe down. Do you want everyone around to hear you?

Wendy looked at Claire realizing how loud she had become. "Oh sorry," Wendy said, grabbing Claire by the hands. "It's just the puzzle pieces are coming together. I mean, even the day he died, he acted bizarre screaming at something invisible in the cell."

Finger Bones caught on and began nodding his head and shaking his finger, leaving Henry alone in his bewilderment. He looked muddled.

"Don't you see, Henry?" Wendy boomed. "You are correct. Lefty Lennie Spinsters was hollering at a ghost the day he tragically died in his cell. Even the day he was captured. He was not crazy. He was scared. And the ghost Lefty Lennie happened to be scared of was 'The Boss'! It was one thing to work for The Boss when he was alive. But to see and work for him as a ghost…deadly."

Henry seemed very pleased with himself. He bowed his chest and looped his thumbs in his front pockets. "I am a genius."

"Yeah right, Henry. Get over it and listen," Claire spat, half-jokingly.

Wendy's face turned serious. "Do you think Lefty Lennie has already left the jail house, Finger Bones? If he returned on the day the cabin burned how does he still have energy? He should be running on empty after all he has done."

"How long does it take for a ghost to gain strength Finger Bones?" Henry asked.

"Oh, it depends. Sometimes it takes a ghost only a few hours to soak up their energy and sometimes it takes days. For example, a person who has led a calm and happy life might not take but five or six hours. A sickly person who knew their time was near may take a day. On the other hand, someone who died a tragic or sudden death, the spook may take days before all the energy is absorbed into their ghostly presence."

"Well, he should be hanging around somewhere near the jail. I believe Lefty Lennie Spinsters' death would be classified as a tragedy," Henry said. "He remained a crazy and infuriated man for the remainder of his life in that cell. And his death was quick."

Finger Bones agreed. "Lefty Lennie could very well be at the jail house or someplace around the vicinity. And you are correct in your thinking, Wendy. He should have used all his energy the night of the fire. That's why I'm concerned. He could go after the next best thing."

"And what's that, Finger Bones?" Wendy asked.

"He could suck the energy from other ghosts."

"Ghosts can absorb energy from other ghosts?" Wendy asked.

Finger Bones smacked his lips, nodded once, and answered, "Yep, they sure can. A ghost can absorb their own energy. But a ghost steals another's energy by literally sucking it out of them. They can't absorb the energy from other ghosts. Oh no, they have to wait until the other ghost absorbs their own energy. Then and only then can they suck the energy out of them."

"That's so sad," Claire said, poking out her lips. "Then the poor ghost couldn't carry out his deed if another ghost stole his energy. What if he wanted to say bye to his wife?"

"What If he wanted to kill his wife?" Henry disputed.

"Guys hush. This is serious," Wendy spat.

Finger Bones looked intently at Wendy, then to Claire, and finally to Henry. "I hope you find him before he can cause such damage. If he has taken energy from ghosts, Lefty Lennie will be a Level 2 ghost. And the more energy he takes the stronger he'll be."

Wendy reached in her pocket for the last piece of gum. Plopping it in her mouth she professed, "Claire. Henry. We've got some thinking to do before Saturday morning. Bright and early we're going to send this ornery ghost, Lefty Lennie Spinsters, back to where he belongs."

Chapter Eighteen

Wendy fidgeted in her desk and propped her head up with a sigh. She peeked impatiently at the clock every five minutes. Claire and Henry were no better off than Wendy. Claire put her head on the desk and blew out a low grunt. Henry tapped his pencil in time with the second hand. He tried counting also. He thought if he could count to sixty several times the time would go faster. Counting in a low whisper, he tapped the metal part of the pencil on the desk. He lost his rhythm after about every ten counts and had to restart when the second hand made it back around to the number twelve.

Wendy watched Miss Ingram as she stood at the front of the classroom facing the chalkboard. She bobbled up and down as she wrote spelling words on the board. About half way through the list she paused. In a calm and clear voice she announced, "Now tonight, boys and girls, you are to write each spelling word five times. So I suggest you began writing them now. The three o'clock bell rings in exactly twenty minutes."

***

A light breeze rustled red, orange, and yellow leaves over the sidewalk onto the trimmed lawn of the courthouse. Wendy, Claire, and Henry trotted swinging their backpacks. Once again, the cool wind blew causing their jackets to flap in the breeze. It was Thursday afternoon after school. Claire and Henry were going to the library with Wendy today.

Wendy and her friends planned to research their topics for their classroom assignment on Bridgeville. They were also going to start on their poster boards for the verbal report. Well, at least until Wendy got off at five. Their main objective was to visit Willie Porter at the train trestle. Wendy hoped he could give some insight into where Lefty Lennie Spinsters might have journeyed, if he wasn't at the jail house. But for the next hour and forty-five minutes they researched information for their papers, jotted down important information in notebooks, and drew out ideas for their posters.

The day before, a delivery truck backed up to the rear parking lot of the library. Wendy had been told about the new computer. A brand new laptop was delivered to the city library. With only one day of practice, Mrs. Taylor clicked and tapped on the computer showing off her new skills. Her aged fingers clicked the mouse with ease. She helped pull up books and newspaper clippings for everyone. Mrs. Taylor also copied the newspaper clippings for Wendy they had researched.

Claire decided to write about a bridge in Bridgeville called the *Crooked Bridge*. Well, it was a bridge. It had recently cracked and had fallen due to high waters and debris flowing down the river.

Henry chose the old jail house for his report. He thought the old structure was one of the spookiest places around besides the old cemetery. And he hadn't dared to go there.

All three friends jumped when the sound of the first strike toned. The five o'clock bell chimed from the courthouse tower. Wendy jumped and heavily marked a squiggly line on her poster board. Claire dropped her pencil and grabbed her chest in fright. Henry twisted in his chair ready to run, but caught himself when Wendy raised her voice.

"Henry, stop!"

Henry blew out a loud breath, "It got us again. I tell you, one day that bell's going to give someone a heart attack."

Wendy gained her composure. She knew it was time. She didn't respond to Henry's remark. She stood and began picking up her books. "Get up you two. Let's get everything cleaned up. It's time to meet Willie."

Chapter Nineteen

The trio pranced down the levee toward the train trestle. They paused at the top of the steps and looked around. Something was different to Wendy. Everything was silent, too silent. The wind had stopped and the trees stood silent. Wendy quietly neared the trestle while Claire and Henry stood back and listened. Wendy softly called out his name. "Willie, are you here?"

Claire took a couple of tiny steps closer to Wendy. Claire then heard a twig snap. "Wendy?"

"It is okay, Claire. See, you stepped on a stick," Wendy said, turning and pointing to the stick close to Claire's feet. Wendy turned back around to face the train trestle. "I know Willie's here. He has to be."

"Maybe we should come back...um...another day. I—I don't th—think he i—is here," Claire stuttered.

A light whiff of cold air blew against the back of Henry's neck. He froze for a split second, but knew his legs had other ideas. He jerked to turn and run, but nothing happened. His feet would not move. He lurched left, and then right, attempting to move. Still, his feet stayed grounded. Henry bent over and twisted. Losing his balance, he threw out his hands to steady himself and to keep from falling. He craved to run, but for some reason his feet would not budge.

"Cut it out, Henry. The way you are acting, Willie may not appear now. You're acting really weird," Wendy scolded, looking back over her shoulder.

"It's not me," Henry whispered in a panicked voice. "I can't move my blooming feet and something is breathing down my neck." Trying to free the upper part of his body, he wobbled back and forth like a teeter totter.

Wendy, being the thinker of the group, knew something wasn't right. She turned to where Henry stood. Her eyes searched all around him. Claire edged over to stand beside Wendy. Shoulder to shoulder both moved toward Henry.

Wendy and Claire stopped. They stood there and stared. For before them they saw a transparent figure of a person, and he stood directly behind Henry. Wendy took a small gulp of air. Claire breathed in sharply, but no sound came out.

Wendy glanced at Claire. "Stay right here and don't you move."

"Don't worry. I will stay. I don't believe I could move if I wanted to at this point."

Wendy looked back at Henry and began to tip toe toward the ghost. "Don't move, Henry. I have a plan."

"Don't move? Have you been listening to me? I can't move," Henry shouted, wiping sweat from his long bangs.

The moment Henry hollered, the figure which bobbled behind him showed itself. Wendy jumped backwards. Claire jumped forwards. They grabbed and hugged each other tightly.

"Hi folks," Willie Porter announced, smiling. He swayed back and forth on his heels. "Glad you all could come by and visit."

Wendy narrowed her eyes. She propped her fists on her hips and stomped both feet. "Willie Porter. That was so not cool. And what's the big deal planting Henry's feet to the ground like roots of a tree?" Wendy scolded.

"Oh, the feet, I can take care of that," Willie said nonchalantly. Taking a handkerchief from his pocket, Willie waved it at Henry's feet. Little balls of light flew from the handkerchief covering Henry's tennis shoes.

Henry looked down at his shoes. He was dazed by what was happening. He thought he was seeing things. Shiny glowing balls flew in many directions around his feet. After a few seconds, one by one the shining balls dwindled away until there were no more. Henry pulled and lifted one foot, and then the other. Guardedly, he turned to meet this Willie Porter who had pranked him.

Willie extended his right hand. He was laughing. "I would like to shake the hand of the person who has managed to make me laugh. I haven't enjoyed myself this much in a very long time."

Not expecting this type of statement, Henry glanced over at Wendy and then back at Willie. Henry shrugged his shoulders and without a word he nodded his head in agreement. They raised their hands to shake, but their hands didn't meet. Willie's ghost hand went straight through Henry's hand.

Willie raised his hand in front of his own face and stared at it. Disappointment washed over him.

Wendy, Claire, and Henry looked at each other in silence. No one knew what to say. Unexpectedly, Claire took several silent steps toward Willie. She extended her hand and reached for the hand Willie held up. A small smile crossed her face and she tilted her head. "Close your eyes. *Feel* the touch of my hand."

Willie looked uncertain.

"You can do it."

He did as she said and closed his eyes.

"Now relax. Allow your shoulders to lower."

Willie wiggled and rotated his shoulders. He then began to relax.

"Good. Now take my hand." Claire gently moved her hand into Willie's hand, and inch-by-inch he lowered his hand inside the embrace of hers. Claire kept her eyes on Willie. He kept his eyes closed.

"Amazing, I can feel your hand holding my hand," Willie said. "It has been so many years since I've felt a human hand. Wow, your hand is so warm."

"Well open your eyes. We are shaking hands," Claire said with a tiny giggle.

Willie opened his eyes. A smile from ear-to-ear gradually covered his face until he was beaming and glowing. "Well, my my my. Look at me. I sure am. Yes I am." He then began to laugh with Claire. Wendy and Henry joined in the laughter.

Claire glanced over at Wendy and said lightheartedly, "I know a couple of things about a ghost myself. I read books too, you know."

When Claire and Willie let go of hands, Wendy decided this was a good time to ask Willie some questions. "Willie, may I ask you some questions?"

"Sure, Wendy."

"Um, do you remember telling me about a ghost who walked out of the river when I saw you last time?"

"Sure, I remember."

"When you were alive do you remember a man named Left Lennie Spinsters? You may have read about him in the Bridgeville Clipper or heard about him from some of the locals."

"I seem to recall a man named Lefty Lennie," Willie answered. He placed a finger on his chin. "Yes, yes, now I remember. That Lefty Lennie was one mean character. He terrorized everyone in Bridgeville and in the surrounding towns too. It was during the 50's. He was one bad man. He sure was."

Wendy was glad Willie recalled this man. "Great, okay, now, was the man who walked out of the river Lefty Lennie Spinsters?"

Willie paused thinking again. Then he eyes went wide in shock. "Oh my gosh! You know what? He *was* Lefty Lennie Spinsters. I thought I knew that face from somewhere."

Wendy looked and Claire and then at Henry. She looked back at Willie trying to stay calm. "Do you know, or, can you find out if he's still at the old jail? It would be a great help if you could."

"I can if you can wait here for about two or three minutes more. I think I know one or two ghosts I can ask."

"Sure, we can wait."

Willie popped out of sight, and returned in less than two minutes. To Wendy it felt like two hours.

When Willie returned, Wendy could tell he was in a grave mood.

"What did you find out?" Wendy asked. Her stomach did flip flops.

"In town there's a ghost named Benedict. He roams the woods behind the old jail house. He was killed in 1977 for two dollars by a drunk. He said Lefty Lennie Spinsters continues to linger at the old jail house at this very moment." Willie looked away.

Only Wendy noticed the troubled look Willie carried on his face. He knew something else and he didn't want to tell. Wendy appreciated Willie helping, so she didn't want to push. "Hey Willie, thanks for going to ask."

"No problem," Willie mumbled, avoiding Wendy's eyes.

"Well, I guess we'd better go. Claire, Henry, our parents will send out a search party if we're late."

"It was a pleasure to meet you, Willie," Claire said, walking up to Willie.

"Yeah, you too," Willie shyly replied.

"I think you're a pretty cool guy. We'll come back soon," Henry said.

The three friends turned to leave. They needed to cross West Street to Golden Hill Road where Claire and Henry lived. Wendy lived two blocks behind them.

Willie stared at the three with his mouth twisted. He shook his head, gave-up, and hollered, "Hey guys, wait. I've one more thing to tell you."

The three stopped. They turned to look at Willie with curiosity. Willie jogged to meet them. "Listen. The ghost I went and talked to earlier. The one named Benedict. He's an old ghost in Bridgeville. He has lingered in those woods behind the old jail for over thirty years. He has seen many ghosts return to Bridgeville to finish their business. He has also heard many things.

Benedict told me one more thing I think you should know. I should have told you before. The ghost you asked me about, Lefty Lennie, he's up to no good. Benedict said there's a dark evil lurking behind Lefty Lennie Spinsters. And Lefty Lennie's here to do his bidding. Be careful my new friends. Benedict smells something big and it will not be long before it arrives."

Chapter Twenty

Saturday morning, Wendy crawled out of bed. She could hear the wintergreen leaves crunch under her pillow. With her eyes half open, she kneeled on the floor and reached under the bed to grab her backpack and clothes. She had prepared them the night before. As she dressed, she checked to make sure she still wore the stringed necklace holding the whistle. She then tiptoed down the stairs and slipped out the back sliding door.

The wind blew lightly. The air smelled of fresh cut grass and sap from the pine trees. A squirrel scurried across the backyard startled from the squishing sound of Wendy's tennis shoes as she walked. It twitched its tail and scrambled up the tree to where the tree house stood. She treaded lightly onto the wet ground. She was careful not to let the rain droplets, dropping periodically from the eaves of the house, splat on her.

Claire and Henry pedaled their bikes across the yard and stopped under the tree house to wait for Wendy. Their backpacks were loaded and ready, strapped over their shoulders. Grasping the handles, Wendy kicked up the kickstand of her bike and rolled it out of the garage. The trio rode down Hardwood Ridge Drive as daylight peaked from around each dark cloud, covering the morning sky. They then turned left onto Screaming Hollow Road.

Although Screaming Hollow Road was a longer route to the old jail, Wendy figured not as many nosey locals traveling through town would spot them if they went down the dirt road. As soon as they neared the cabin, she applied the brakes on her bike. She jumped off the seat and gazed at Finger Bones' cabin. Claire and Henry pulled up behind her. Wendy remembered the last time she had stood in this spot. Finger Bones was alive and the cabin was standing with smoke rising to the sky from the chimney.

It laid in ruins now. A small one roomed house with a fireplace, Finger Bones had called home. Wendy felt sad seeing the charred walls propped on the ground burned and broken.

The smell of smoke filled Wendy's nostrils. It reminded her of the job that lay ahead for the morning. She turned to Claire and Henry. "Thank you both for helping me through this. Are you both ready? Do you really want to do this?"

Claire looked at Wendy. "Listen, Henry and I are your friends. I'm ready. Whoever or whatever did this to Finger Bones needs to be stopped. Plus, you have an important job to do in this town, Wendy. And you chose us to help you."

Wendy raised her eyebrows. "When did you become so brave?"

"I'm in too." Henry said solemnly, holding out a hand. He looked up at Claire.

Claire slapped a hand on top of his. "I don't know if I am so brave. But, no one messes with my best friends and Finger Bones is included. I'm in."

Wendy joined her friends. The three took turns adding their hands to the pile as they had many times. Then together they chanted, "Through thick and thin, friends till the end."

It was typical for fog to roll in and linger after a good rain. The foggy mist snaked its way from the river to the sides of the building giving the now vacant jail an even more eerie appearance. The bikes were dumped a block away from the old jail house. Wendy, Claire, and Henry entered the front gate leading up to the stone steps. Silently, the three crept through the already missing front door.

Upon entering, they entered a dark hall. Immediately to the left was an office and to the right another short hall. Wendy could tell the short hall turned left at the end. Wendy decided to course straight ahead. After several small steps, she ducked to keep her arm from grazing a dangling spider web.

Wendy glanced back to see if Claire and Henry were behind her. They were. She held her hand up for them to stop. She wanted to allow time for their eyes to adjust to the dark. She pointed to them and then to her ears. She wanted them to listen. They heard nothing but silence.

Wendy looked ahead after her vision adjusted to the darkness. Several feet ahead on the left she noticed were three cells. She motioned for Claire and Henry to stay put. Pointing straight ahead, she prodded forward to check the cells.

Henry lightly nudged Claire to follow Wendy. Claire jumped. And though Henry couldn't see great in the dark, he could see well enough to know not to startle her again.

"I'm sorry," he mouthed, also deciding the spot where they stood for the moment was best. Wendy could check out the jail cells.

A single undersized window held four vertical bars at the rear of each cell. A dim light flowed through the desolate cells settling on the now empty bunk beds. Wendy reached and pulled a flashlight from her backpack. Shining the flashlight toward the dark corners, she didn't see anything. As she reached out to grab one of the heavy cell doors, Wendy heard a loud creaking sound followed by an echo coming from another room in the jail.

After a brief silence, Wendy heard the noise again. This noise sounded as though it were coming from upstairs. Wendy tiptoed back to where Claire and Henry stood. By the looks on their faces, they had heard it too. The noise came a third time. It turned into a faint whirling wind, and it was growing stronger. No, not just wind, it was a slurping sound mixed with a whirling wind sound.

Carefully, they edged down the short hall, and then turned to the left. Ten feet ahead were stairs of stone ascending to the right.

Wendy ascended the steps with Claire and Henry at her heels. Halfway they paused on a platform. The steps turned once more to the right and then led to the second floor. By the time they reached the last step, the sound turned earsplitting.

Wendy, Claire, and Henry cautiously stepped onto the second floor. Wendy gazed around the large room. Single jail cells wrapped around three of the four walls. The deafening sound continued, but no one saw anything but cell bars.

From the dimness at the far end of the room, Wendy spotted a darker shadow flickering on the wall. She held up a hand for Claire and Henry to stay put and pointed toward the movement.

Wendy took a small gulp of air and walked toward the shadow. She thought her ears would burst the noise became so loud. The darkness became brighter as she neared and soon an object came into view.

Chapter Twenty-one

There he stood, Lefty Lennie Spinsters, holding a helpless soul in his grip, ruthlessly sucking the energy from his ghostly body. Wendy stood dismayed. She realized they were not prepared for a Level Two ghost. She turned and looked at Claire and Henry, but she decided to stay quiet for now.

The drained ghost, which Lefty Lennie had gripped around the neck, carried a horrific look on his face. His colorless mouth hung wide open. Wendy could see a powdery black substance drifting and floating from the victimized ghost into Lefty Lennie's opened mouth. Both seemed to be in a trance. Lefty Lennie held the ghost at eye level effortlessly sucking and slurping the helpless soul's energy.

Wendy walked backwards a few feet. She then slowly pulled the backpack from her shoulders and sat it on the floor. She knew after a ghost had sucked the energy form another their strength increased. She wondered how long it would take for the energy to take effect. She reached in and pulled out the bag containing the salt. Looking over at the wide-eyed Claire and jittery looking Henry, she pointed to the salt, and then pointed in the direction where Lefty Lennie stood in the dark shadows. Wendy made a circular motion in the air with her finger.

Claire cupped a shaky hand and whispered to Henry, "Remember, the circle of salt bounds a ghost and entraps him."

Claire looked at Wendy and gave her a thumbs-up.

Good, she understood, Wendy thought. *Oh my, her face looks horrified.* Wendy decided Henry's face looked no better and his legs shook to the point she thought she heard them rattle. Wendy was proud of them though. They were still here.

"She's going to circle it around Lefty Lennie. Let's move up a little in case she needs us," Claire whispered to Henry.

Henry nodded in agreement.

Taking cautious steps, Wendy squatted and sprinkled a solid, salt circle around Lefty Lennie Spinsters. Luckily, she accomplished this task just in time. The sucking slurping sound turned to a faster, high pitched sound. After three or four seconds more, it stopped.

Wendy rushed toward Claire and Henry. All three stared at Lefty Lennie, wiping his mouth with his free hand while slinging the drained ghost to the floor with the other hand.

Lefty Lennie smacked his lips. A gratifying smile covered his face. As a ray of light made its way through the room, his bloodshot eyes shimmered. Lefty Lennie leaned back and threw his arms up and out. His voice roared out for all ghosts to hear. The energy flowed through his body making him stronger.

Next to him in a pile on the floor, the other ghost lay shriveled and dried. Across his face, the withered ghost still carried a look of terror. They gaped at the cold-bloodedness of this cruel ghost, Lefty Lennie Spinsters.

Unknowingly, Wendy shifted her feet kicking a pebble backwards until it fell down the stairs with an echo. Lefty Lennie Spinsters snapped from his trance. He turned swiftly facing the trio. A look of surprise spread across his face.

He narrowed his eyes and growled. "Well, what do we have here?" He looked down discovering the bag of salt gripped tightly in Wendy's hands. He gave a humorous laugh, his menacing look intimidating. "Are you kidding me?" he snarled. "You are now the chosen one? You're nothing but a child. A child cannot capture me."

Wendy took offense at his words. "Well, the way I see it, you're already captured." Claire and Henry hurried to stand beside Wendy. All three glanced down at the salt, which circled Lefty Lennie's feet.

Lefty Lennie bent his large head down. Upon seeing the circle of salt, he became enraged. "How dare you." He raised his fist over his head swinging down with force, but his fist stopped in midair with a loud thud by an invisible barrier. He became more enraged. He shrieked and growled. He kicked with his left foot, then with his right, but as hard as he tried he could not break through the seal of salt.

Wendy breathed in a sigh of relief. She knew Lefty Lennie could not break through the circle of salt, at least for now.

"Hurry, Claire, reach in and pull out the paper and write down Lefty Lennie's full name," Wendy ordered. "Henry, take out the glass soda bottle. Claire when you finish writing down the name, roll the paper and stuff it in the bottle."

Claire and Henry set into motion, jerking the backpacks from their shoulders, unzipping compartments, and grabbing for their items. Claire snatched out a piece of wrinkled notebook paper and a half broken pencil, scribbling the name

Lefty Lennie Spinsters on one side. She then rolled it and stuffed it into the bottle as fast as she could.

"Okay, I did it," Claire shouted.

"Good job," Wendy yelled. "Now, Claire, pour in the graveyard dirt and cork the top." Henry tightly held the bottle while Claire poured the graveyard dirt and corked the top.

"Finished," Henry announced relieved, swinging around to show Wendy.

"I am depending on you two," Wendy said. "Get the bottle to Bone River. Throw it as hard as you can to the deepest part."

Claire and Henry turned to run, but suddenly stopped. Something behind them made a thud. Henry knew before he turned. He forgot to zip his backpack and the old baseball his brother had given him hit the floor. No sound could be heard but the bouncing of the baseball rolling straight toward the circle of salt. Watching in horror, the three stood in awkward positions. They resembled still shots in a movie. Their eyes turned into saucers. The ball slid to a halt just inside the circle. To their dismay, the ball left behind an opened mark in the salt.

"Oh no," Claire whimpered. "I knew this wasn't a good idea."

Wendy and her two friends stared at the baseball. A tapping noise began. It was Lefty Lennie tapping his foot. The three moved their eyes from the baseball to Lefty Lennie's shoes. They gazed to his striped pants up to his waist. Lefty Lennie had balled his hand into a fist, slamming it into his other hand. They swallowed and gawked further up to where a smile of triumph smeared across his face.

"Run!" Wendy yelled.

Claire and Henry whirled and ran as fast as their legs would carry them. The bottle was held tightly in Henry's grip in one hand and his backpack clutched in the other. Claire slung her backpack over one shoulder and took the rear in a sprint. She stayed close behind Henry. Both skipped two and three steps at a time as they descended the stone stairs slamming into the wall on the first floor. Claire and Henry regained their momentum and dashed to the front of the jail. They stormed out the front door, scampered around the building, and headed for Bone River. Neither realized Wendy was not following behind them.

His eyes crinkled down on the sides. Seeing Wendy helpless, no friends around, and no Finger Bones, Lefty Lennie's smile grew so wide his lips curled up. The fresh new energy in him made him stronger, more egotistical, and his confidence heightened to new levels. Taking his time, he slid a foot over the break in the circle. Disturbed dust settled on his old black boots.

Wendy slowly slid to the left. She knew she had to think fast. There was no time for bubblegum this time and the less movements she made the better. She stared into his bloodshot eyes. His eyes did not blink. Behind her she groped for the rail. Wendy hoped he didn't notice. She clenched the rail which led to the stairs. She felt she had a better chance outside.

Wendy slowly felt her way to the end of the rail. She paused to make sure she had her footing. Wendy then reeled around and rushed down the stairs. Her backpack flopped with each stair she jumped. She could hear an enraged Left Lennie Spinsters striding across the floor upstairs as she flew out the front door. His black boots pounded the floor as he rocked from side to side in pursuit.

The shoelace to Wendy's right foot freed, causing her to stumble down the last step of the old jail. She fell hitting and scrapping her knee. Inside, the roar of the giant ghost poured down the stairs. Wendy quickly examined the knee, brushed it with one stroke, and sprang up running.

Her bad luck did not stop there. Running out the gate and turning, Wendy snagged her jacket on the fence, jerking and slamming her against the fence. Something caught in her pants legs. Wendy glanced down and saw she was standing in catnip plants. Clinging to one of the stems with blooms was a red balloon. A single red balloon had fallen from Henry's backpack.

"Hum, maybe my luck is changing," Wendy said, allowing a small smile. The catnip grew across the entire gate along the foot of the fence. She plucked several hairy stems with blooms and a few of the large heart shaped leaves. Grabbing the red balloon, Wendy ran to the side of the building where an outside water faucet was located. Turning on the faucet, Wendy filled the balloon with water. Next to the faucet, a ladder climbed the wall to a balcony on the second floor. Wendy scurried up a ladder.

A black iron fence edged the borders of the balcony, which overlooked the front porch and steps of the jail. Wendy darted over to the edge preparing her idea. She heard the whales of Lefty Lennie penetrate the air. "Okay you big, overgrown baboon. Just wait until you get a mouthful of this,"

Wendy murmured, bending down on one knee, and then shifting to the other knee so as not to lean on the scrapped one.

Fortunately, the big baboon ran slower than a snapping turtle and just as awkward. It gave her the time she needed. Wendy broke the blossom off the stem and hurriedly broke up the leaves. She crumbled them and stuffed the pieces into the opening of the balloon. Some pieces floated and some sank down into the water. Wendy tied off the balloon, jumped up, and readied herself in position. She waited.

"Where are you? I'll get you and when I do..." Wendy stopped talking. The big baboon suddenly appeared below where she stood on the balcony.

He stormed to the edge of the porch. He looked from left, to right, but didn't look up. The ghostly figure swayed from foot to foot and growled loudly, "You rotten kid, I'll snap your neck!"

Wendy leaned over the rail. She stretched out her arm and held the balloon up high. "Hey blubber butt, up here!" Wendy yelled, cupping her mouth with her other hand.

The snarling Lefty Lennie Spinsters bent his large head back looking straight up at Wendy. He turned so angry the tops of his ears turned red and his eyes bulged like those of a slithering iguana.

Wendy smiled. Waving with one hand, she held up the balloon filled with water and catnip with the other. "Hey pumpkin head, I have a little present for you!"

'Infuriated' was not a good word for the expression Lefty Lennie Spinsters carried on his face, for when Wendy spoke he flung out his arms and roared at the top of his lungs.

She knew the timing had to be perfect. At the moment his head bent backwards and his mouth opened, Wendy let go of the balloon. "BINGO!" shouted Wendy. "I got a hole in one!"

The balloon landed perfectly, hitting the back of his throat. The catnip coated his vocal cords and silenced his roar. The catnip quickly flowed throughout the rest of his ghostly body. Lefty Lennie started making a choking sound. He staggered around on the porch with his large hands wrapped around his neck. He looked shocked. The effect of whatever he had swallowed began to show. His eyes slowly batted. They closed little by little until sleep overpowered him and he dropped to the concrete porch.

"Nighty night," Wendy said, waving to the overgrown Lefty Lennie.

Lefty Lennie Spinsters lay in a scrunched up ball with a fat thumb crammed in his mouth. His eyes smiled as he sucked on his thumb making gooey noises.

Wendy looked over the rail. "Well, what about that! It worked." Her face turned from shocked to happy. She began bouncing up and down with delight. "Hotdog, it really worked!"

"We did it Wendy!" Claire and Henry shouted, jogging around the building.

"Hey, where are you, Wendy?" Henry called out, slowing at the gate.

"Up here, Henry," Wendy hollered, waving her arms.

Claire and Henry turned their eyes toward the balcony where Wendy stood waving and jumping. She pointed below to the porch. Their eyes followed her direction. On the porch, the big tough guy called Lefty Lennie Spinsters lay curled up like a newborn baby. As the three looked upon this goofy sight, the large overgrown Lefty Lennie slowly disappeared. He vanished right before their eyes until there was nothing but a water puddle, dripping onto the top step of the old jail in Bridgeville.

Chapter Twenty-two

The day arrived for Wendy and her classmates to present their reports. White posters littered the walls and desks. Nervous bodies fidgeted and squirmed in their seats. Wendy's throat suddenly felt very dry. She gazed around the room at the mayhem. Leon Brady, one of the smartest kids in the classroom, flipped through his index cards while he mouthed his speech. Wendy noticed his hands were trembling as he shoved one card behind the other. Duke Gideon turned and bent over to the floor desperately trying to catch a page from his report. It had flown off his desk and slid under Emily Dean's.

A table had been placed in the front of the classroom that morning, and a project display board was placed on top. When the class returned after lunch, Mrs. Ingram stood beside the table and began writing each student's name on slip of paper. She then folded each one and dropped them into a hat.

There was a moment of silence as the children waited nervously.

She swirled the hat. "Okay everyone, you know how this works. I draw a name from the hat. The person's name drawn should bring their materials with them to the front of the room to present their report. You can pin your posters here on the display board."

Taking the hat in her hands once again, she swirled it, reached in, and pulled out a name. "Our first report will be given by...Polly Napper."

Wendy thought Henry was lucky. Miss Ingram called his name second. Claire at least made the top ten, being number eight. However, she ended up being the last name drawn. So by the time her turn rolled around it was late in the school day.

She picked up her index cards and grabbed her poster board. It was a drawing from the waist up of Lefty Lennie

Spinsters. *I should have drawn the ghost of him,* she thought as she meandered to the front. *My friends would have thought that was cool. But if they had seen the real ghost, I imagine a few would have changed their minds.* She giggled. *They would have run like scared chickens.*

She placed her cards on the podium. Everyone had turned in their typed reports that morning. About the time she twisted around to pin the poster up, Wendy heard a noise coming from the back of the room. It was a hissing sound. As she held it in place on the display board, she turned to look.

She saw nothing unusual, but sixteen pairs of eyes watching her. Wendy turned back around to finish pinning the poster.

Again, she heard the noise. This time it sounded like one of her classmates, trying to get her attention. "Psst, hey Wendy, over here."

"Who is calling me?" she asked annoyed, and getting aggravated with the pins.

"It's me. I'm right back here."

Wendy whirled around. "Who's me and..." Her eyes widened and her jaw dropped. Standing in the very back of the room was Willie Porter.

"Wendy whenever you're ready you may begin," Miss Ingram said, sitting in one of the empty desks among the kids.

Wendy didn't respond or move. She stood there, frozen, staring at the ghost. Several of the classmates began whispering and giggling. Others turned in their desks to see what she was gawking at in the back of the room. However, no one could see the ghost, except her. This time, not even Claire or Henry could see him.

Wendy shook her head. She tried to think. She had to somehow tell Claire and Henry to look to the back where

Willie stood. She patted her pocket. *Ah, my bubblegum. I sure wish I could chew it right now.*

Claire looked over at Henry. He shrugged his shoulders back at her.

Wendy had an idea. Making it look like an accident, she turned toward the display table once more and purposely rammed her foot into the leg of it. The display board, along with her poster board, plummeted to the ground. Wendy's face turned beet red. "Ouch, that hurt!" she groaned under her breath.

Stooping to the floor, she glanced at Claire and then at Henry. Both jumped from their desk to help her. They bent to their knees in front of Wendy.

"Are you okay, Wendy?" Claire whispered.

"I know you're nervous Wendy, but it's not so bad. My voice cracked only three times," Henry added.

Wendy stared at the ground. "Ssshhh! It's not the speech. Look toward the back of the room. Willie Porter's standing in the back."

They whipped around to see.

"Where?" Henry asked, looking around to the back of the classroom. "I don't see him."

"I don't see him either," Claire said. "Are you sure?"

"Yes, I'm sure. Can't you see him? He's standing between Nate and Paul," Wendy retorted, pointing to the back of the room.

Miss Ingram had four rows of desks in her room. Nate Little and Paul Ward sat in the middle rows in the back.

Claire and Henry glanced once more. They didn't see Willie Porter.

Henry looked at Wendy. "Wendy, I don't see anyone, dead or alive, standing behind Nate and Paul."

"Well, I'm telling you both. He's standing there. And he's waving at me," Wendy snapped through gritted teeth.

"Calm down, we believe you," Claire said.

Wendy looked back at Willie. Her face changed from a frustrated look to a panicked look. "Something's wrong. I know it. Willie's not waving anymore and he looks scared."

"Maybe someone's after him," Henry suggested.

"What if it's Lefty Lennie Spinsters," Claire cried.

"No way, we got rid of that loser two weeks ago," he answered.

"It's true, Claire. I don't think his coming back," Wendy said.

Wendy heard Buck Fergus laughing in the back with his two buddies, Duke and Paul. The three boys seemed to be taking great satisfaction in trying to humiliate Wendy.

Buck began talking in a whiney voice. "Oh, please don't make me give this report. I'm so afraid. Oh wait. Maybe I can do it if my friends hold my hand." Sliding down in their chairs, the three boys grabbed their stomachs and burst out laughing.

"Shut your big mouth, Buck," Henry growled angrily.

"Boys, that's enough. Buck, your remark just gained you one week of break detention. Another remark and I'll give you two," Miss Ingram said firmly. "Claire and Henry, thank you for helping Wendy. Now please be seated so we can continue."

"Oh no," Wendy panicked.

"What's happening?" Claire asked, fearful of what Wendy would say.

"I don't know. He's beginning to fade away. And it looks like he's on fire," she said bewildered.

Willie was literally fizzing away like a fuse on a firecracker. His body was sparking and firing, and he was gradually disappearing from sight.

"His power grows stronger, Wendy," Willy said in agonizing pain.

Wendy made up her mind. She knew her classmates would think her crazy, but Willie needed her help. She had to talk to him. Wendy jumped up and hollered, "Willie, whose body is growing stronger? What's happening?"

The entire class stopped laughing. All heads turned to see who this Willie was. But all they saw was the empty space.

"It's Lefty Lennie Spinsters," Willie said in a faint voice. "He is up to no good I tell you. Wendy, we need you at the cemetery by dark. I heard them say their conjuring The Boss on the Full Moon." Willie stopped talking. He held his hands out in front of him. "Oh my, look at me," he said too

252

calmly. He twisted his hands back and forth. "It's already happening."

"What?" Wendy said, making a gasping sound.

"Ghosts who are not willing to change for this cruel spirit will face punishing deeds such as this," he said, looking at Wendy, and then back at his hands. "We will stay strong and try to hang on until you get there."

His eyes told a different story. He looked frightened as he watched his hands fizz away and then his arms. He looked up and over at Wendy once more. "Hurry Wendy, he has Mrs. Harper," Willie managed to grunt out before his mouth and then his head fizzed away. Then all of a sudden, *POW!*

Wendy let out a terrifying gasp. "I don't believe it." She stood there staring at the spot where Willie had stood. "He has Mrs. Harper? It's my fault. I should've been prepared for Lefty Lennie the first time. Finger Bones tried to tell me he was gaining strength. I waited too long to go after him."

Claire and Henry jumped up and ran over to stand beside Wendy.

"Wendy?" Henry asked. "What happened to Willie?

"Who has Mrs. Harper?" Claire sobbed.

"And what is this mumbo jumbo that it's your fault?" Henry asked concerned.

"He fizzed away and blew up like a firecracker," Wendy said stunned. "I should have been more prepared the first time." She looked down at her own hands. "Willie said The Boss will return on the Full Moon. I need to get to the cemetery by dark. He also said Lefty Lennie has Mrs. Harper." Wendy blinked a couple of times, looking around the classroom.

She had forgotten all about her classmates. Luckily, everyone was still staring toward the back of the room. All were looking down at the old wooden floor. There was a large burnt spot embedded in the wood, and it was still smoking.

And a large cloud of smoke was rising up and spreading across the ceiling.

"Wendy, you've got to get out of here," Claire said in a low voice. "The full moon is tonight. Remember, we went over the moon phases in our last section on planets. It will be full at exactly nine thirty-three tonight."

"This was not your fault, Wendy. This isn't over yet. We *will* get him this time. And when we do, we'll send him far away," Henry said reassuringly.

Wendy shook her head, clearing it. She listened to her friends. She knew she had to get it together. She needed to think so she could help Willie, Mrs. Harper, and whoever else was in this mad and crazy plan of the ghosts. She just couldn't understand why Mrs. Harper of all people had been taken by Lefty Lennie, and whoever else was involved. She knew there was only one way to find out.

She looked back over at Miss Ingram. "Um, Miss Ingram, I don't know what all you saw or heard for the last ten minutes, and I don't know how to explain what just happened."

Miss Ingram and the students turned simultaneously in their seats and looked at Wendy.

Wendy awkwardly forced a smile and waved at everyone. Miss Ingram looked shocked and everyone else stared with wide eyes in a daze. Wendy knew her teacher hadn't heard a word she had said. So she thought it best to start again. "Miss Ingram, I, um, don't really know how to explain what just happened. I don't really know myself." She paused, biting her bottom lip. She looked at Claire, at Henry, and then back at her teacher. "And I don't imagine you're going to like or understand what I have to say next. So I apologize in advance." She closed her eyes and took a breath. She then opened her eyes and said bluntly, "Miss Ingram, I really have to go." And that was it. Without another word, Wendy turned and walked out of the classroom door.

Miss Ingram and the students turned their gaze to Claire and Henry.

Claire and Henry smiled a rather large, fake smile.

"She meant the bathroom, you know. Wendy had to go to the bathroom," Henry said, trying to sound casual.

Claire grabbed him by the arm and agreed. "Yes, she did. And I think Henry and I need to go check on her."

"Wendy does this all the time," he said, making the situation worse. "She goes to the bathroom."

Claire pulled Henry by the arm while jerking her head sideways in the direction of the door. She was trying to get him out of the classroom before he said more. "Come on, Henry. I need to check on Wendy. She might be sick and need my help," she hinted, raising her eyebrows. "You can stand guard in the hallway." Henry didn't move. So she tugged on him again. This time she yanked him past her and then pushed him towards the door.

"Oh yeah, sure," he said, snapping his fingers and pointing toward the door. "We are going now to check on her."

"Oh, good grief! Move it, Henry," Claire said, shoving him again.

Chapter Twenty-three

Wendy ran out the school doors and down the steps. She grabbed the piece of bubblegum from her pocket and plopped it in her mouth. She stuffed the wrapper in her pocket and jogged to the bikes. Grabbing the handlebars of her bike, she hopped on, and pedaled away.

She rode as fast as her legs would go. Thinking as she chewed, she decided to take the long way home. Instead of turning right to go home by Screaming Hollow Road, Wendy flew left on Ann Street. She figured this way home she would be less likely to run into any ghosts along the way. Plus, she needed to go by the library and tell Mrs. Taylor she wouldn't be there for work today. She sure hoped she could get in and out fast. She didn't want to have to explain about a ghost kidnapping Mrs. Taylor's sister.

At the very moment she was going to cross the road to go to the library, Wendy caught a glimpse of the blue lights on top of the police car parked at the police station. She slid to a stop. Her dad was standing by the vehicle and was motioning for her to come over. She knew she needed to go by the library and then get home as soon as possible. But she had this odd feeling in the pit of her stomach that what her dad had to say was important. So she crossed the road and pulled up beside him.

"Hey Dad, what's with the blue lights?" she asked.

Mr. Winkelmann opened the door to the police car, reached in, and switched off the blue flashing lights. "Hey, Wendy," he said, standing back up. "Listen, I need to tell you something and I'm asking you not to say anything to anybody about it. Okay?"

"Yes sir."

"I wanted to let you know, Mrs. Taylor closed the library for the rest of the afternoon. I just talked to her on the phone. She's at the Rubottom Plantation. It seems Mrs. Harper is missing."

Wendy didn't think about Mrs. Taylor finding out so soon about her sister. She knew she couldn't tell her dad the truth about where Mrs. Harper was and who had her. Even if she did tell him, he wouldn't believe her. She knew she had to handle this without her dad and it included saving Mrs. Harper.

She thought back to the day Finger Bones shot Lefty Lennie with the special gun. Wendy wanted to go get help on that day, but Finger Bones knew it wouldn't work. "No one's going to believe us, Wendy." He had said.

Mr. Winkelmann had been talking and trying to tell Wendy something while she thought and reminisced. Before he said it for the third time, he cleared his throat loudly.

Wendy snapped out of her thoughts and looked at her dad. "Oh, I'm sorry."

"I said you don't have to work today. Mrs. Taylor locked the doors before she left. You can ride your bike on to the house. Since your mom is the president of the Paws and Pals Club, she has gone over to the animal shelter. Someone found a litter of abandoned puppies and she's meeting the vet there. She said she may be a while, so you can find plenty of microwaveable pizzas, and macaroni and cheese in the kitchen. Sorry, looks like I have to work late too."

"Oh it's okay," Wendy said relieved. "I'll be fine." She felt better not having to make up a story about going somewhere. "Um, Dad, how does Mrs. Taylor know her sister is missing?"

Mr. Winkelmann situated his police cap on his head. "Well, she told me she has been trying to get in touch with her since lunchtime and no one has answered the phone. So about thirty minutes ago she decided to drive out to RuBottom Plantation to check on her. She said she wasn't there, but her van was out in the garage. When she went inside she saw that her keys, purse, and even an umbrella she totes were still in their usual spot at the house."

"Maybe she rode to town with somebody else."

"I asked Mrs. Taylor that too. She says that Mrs. Harper still wouldn't leave her purse or the keys. The keys to the house are on the key ring." Mr. Winkelmann paused. "Hang on." He leaned into the police car again and brought out a small box.

Wait until I get my hands on that crappy ghost. Why would he kidnap such a defenseless old lady?

"Before I forget, Mrs. Taylor asked me if I would go by The Bridgeville Jewel Box and pick this up for her." He pulled the lid from the box and showed Wendy a gold pocket watch. "She says it's very important that you take the watch. You know anything about this?"

Wendy recognized the watch instantly. "Oh my gosh, the gift to Mrs. Harper is the watch Lefty Lennie Spinsters wants after all." Goosebumps covered her arms and legs. "I've been right all along. That's the reason they kidnapped Mrs. Harper."

"What are you talking about?"

Wendy looked at her dad. "Oh nothing. I – I'm just rambling," she stammered. "Mrs. Taylor got the watch for Mrs. Harper's birthday." Wendy had no idea what to do with the watch. Nevertheless, she took the box from her dad and placed it inside her jacket.

Wendy thought it best to keep her dad or anyone else away from the cemetery until Lefty Lennie and The Boss were gone. The ghosts might try to snatch someone else. Maybe if she could name enough places Mrs. Harper went to each week, everyone would stay busy searching for her on this side of town and stay away from Screaming Hollow Road.

"She could be anywhere in town. Why don't you drive over to The Coffee Shop? She goes over there to play bridge once a week."

"I've already called. She never made it to the restaurant, or to the jewelry store."

"What about the beauty salon? Um, they call it The Magic Mirror."

"We've called them and most of the other stores here in Bridgeville. So far, no one has seen her today. Mrs. Taylor was the last person to see her and that was around seven this morning."

Wendy turned her head in the direction of the library doors. Everything was happening all at once. She blew a bubble and before she could pop it, the bubble popped on her face. "Keep looking, Dad. I'm sure she's around town somewhere."

Mr. Winkelmann nodded and got into the police car. "You be careful riding to the house."

"I will. And tell Mrs. Taylor I'm sure her sister will be home soon."

Her dad nodded and then backed out of the parking space. He switched on the blue lights, turned right on West Street, and headed south to the Rubottom Plantation where the sisters lived.

Chapter Twenty-four

Wendy went left and headed home. She jumped the Rail Road tracks pedaling north on West Street. *I think it's strange. They named a road traveling north and south, West Street. I guess it is on the west side of town. So that's what they mean when they say you need to laugh at the little things.* Wendy smiled and pedaled faster.

She traveled up the hill and turned right on Hardwood Ridge Drive. Wendy lived at the end of the road. She coasted down a steep hill and through a sharp curve to the left. Her house was the last one on the right. Located behind it was Bone River.

As she pedaled toward her house, Wendy was in deep thought. All the information she had received over the last couple of weeks flooded her mind like the summary of a movie. Lefty Lennie Spinsters trying to find a watch, Mrs. Taylor finding the special watch, Mrs. Grapples engraving the

267

bizarre poem on the watch many years ago, and now the person who owned the watch was missing. How did it all connect? "I'm going to call Finger Bones."

Wendy dropped her bike to the ground under the tree house and hurried up the ladder. She knew she was going to need her backpack of supplies before heading to the cemetery. But before that she needed some advice. She pulled the whistle out from under her shirt and blew as hard as she could. Finger Bones popped into the room.

"Finger Bones, I'm glad to see you. Have you heard about Mrs. Harper?"

"Yes, I have heard. I see Willie got the message to you."

"He did. Then he fizzed away like a lit sparkler standing right there in the back of the classroom. He said it's what happens when you don't change and do as Lefty Lennie wants, and whoever else is behind this. But I don't know where Willie went," she said concerned.

Finger Bones placed a hand gently on her shoulder. "For now, focus on your job of catching Lefty Lennie. I will be with you every step of the way," he said reassuringly.

Wendy looked up at Finger Bones. "I may be scared, but I'm mad too," she said narrowing her eyes. "They were wrong to take Mrs. Harper. I know she has to be so scared."

"Ah, well, you might be surprised. Mrs. Harper has ways of taking care of herself." He stepped back two steps. "You finish gathering your supplies. I am going to return to the graveyard."

"Wait! I wanted to let you know I have the watch. My dad picked it up for Mr. Taylor. She thinks I know what to do with it."

"Bring it with you. When the time is right, you will know." Finger Bones then popped out of sight.

Wendy stood for a moment confused. White fog twirled around her left behind from Finger Bones departure. "Hey, that was not an answer," she grunted, swatting at the fog.

Wendy grabbed her bag, removed the watch from her jacket, and placed it safely inside the backpack. She then turned and headed toward the trapdoor.

"Where do you think you are going all by yourself?" Henry asked, peeking up at Wendy through the trapdoor.

Wendy jumped backed startled and made a tiny squeal.

"I say she's not going anywhere without us, Henry," Claire said bluntly, opening the trapdoor wider and ignoring her cry. She looked at Wendy and cocked her head to the side. "Friends stick together."

Wendy stared back at the two and took a quick breath. "I know, Claire. I'm sorry for running out. But all I could think about was Mrs. Harper. I couldn't believe someone could be so mean."

"I know," Henry said. "Even for a ghost, taking an old lady is just cruel."

"Yeah, it is." Wendy scooted back so Claire and Henry could climb up. "Thank you guys for coming."

"You're welcome," Claire said. "What do we need to do?"

"I need to tell you some important things while we're up here," Wendy said. "Plus, I have something to show you. Oh, and I just thought about a couple of more items we may need to carry in our backpacks. So we need to open the trunk."

Wendy talked. Claire and Henry sat with their eyes wide and mouths gaped open as Wendy spilled the story about Lefty Lennie Spinsters appearing those afternoon hours before Finger Bones died. She told how angry Lefty Lennie had acted upon spotting her on the dirt road, charging after her on a cloud, and screaming for the watch.

"When he came tromping towards me, I closed my eyes ready for the impact," Wendy said, ducking her head as she talked. "Instead, I heard a loud bang. I opened my eyes, and saw Finger Bones holding a pistol with smoke boiling out the end. He had shot Lefty Lennie with a special gun loaded with bullets, packed with sea salt."

While talking, Wendy removed the key from around her neck and opened the trunk. She then felt over the rough wood and the aged metal with the palms of her hand. Again she found the plain etched star. A shifting sound was heard. The star became a bright golden color and the tray started to rise from the trunk.

"Finger Bones knew the gun would slow Lefty Lennie, but not send him on to his next place. The salt acts as a deterrent. Shooting a ghost with salt, forces the ghost to dissipate for a short period of time."

"That had to hurt," Henry said. "By dissipate, don't you mean it scattered Lefty Lennie all over the place?"

"Yes Henry, dissipate means strewn or scattered. He started to vanish and then all of the sudden he blew up and scattered into a million dark pieces."

Wendy removed Finger Bones' journal and her journal which had been hidden in the secret compartment at the bottom of the trunk. Flipping through the pages, she searched for the page containing the levels of ghosts. I should have paid more attention to the levels last time. I knew when we saw Lefty Lennie holding and sucking the energy from the other ghost he was a Level Two ghost. I had hoped the energy hadn't taken affect so fast."

Claire placed a hand on Wendy's shoulder. "Wendy, you tell me often to stop being so hard on myself. Now I'm giving the advice to you."

"She is right, Wendy. We're all new at this. Now read the journal. We're going ghost hunting," Henry said.

Wendy looked at her two friends. She then picked up Finger Bones' journal and went to work. "We need Level Two ghosts' supplies." Wendy ran her finger up and down the pages. "Here it is. It says:

'Level Two ghosts are transparent most of the time, but can choose to become solid in form as they become stronger. Sometimes they appear fuzzy when scared or upset. They can suck the energy from other ghosts, making themselves stronger. Stronger ghosts no longer need to travel on a cloud. They are becoming more human in appearance and walk on the ground instead. A Level Two ghost can transform into a fog or mist. Anywhere you see fog rolling into an area there is sure to be a Level Two ghost very near.'"

Henry leaned over the trunk spotting a box labeled obsidian stones. The box lay beside where the book was kept. "I didn't see this last time," Henry said.

"Get the box out and open it," Wendy said.

274

Henry slid the top from the box. Five shiny black stones lay in the bottom.

Wendy scrunched her eyes, wondering what the stones were used for. She looked back at the book and turned the page. "Okay, the next part tells how to capture and send Level Two ghosts to their next destination. Henry, do you see a drawer with pine needles and one with sage?"

Henry searched. He found the pine needles and sage already crushed and in three small bags tied with a string. "Got them right here, now what?" He set the bags down.

"Is there a bowl in the trunk? It should be made of pottery. We have to mix the needles and sage, and then burn it. Burning the two ingredients together absorbs negativity from the ghost."

Claire jumped up and looked in one of the drawers in the tree house. "Here are some matches I put in here last year when we popped firecrackers."

"Yep, I found it. Here's the bowl." Henry said, pulling out the bowl.

"Let me read the rest of this in the journal," Wendy said, finding her place.

'Instead of trapping the ghost with the salt, Level Two ghosts have to be trapped with the obsidian stones. You must surround the ghost with the stones. The needles and sage are burned while the ghost is trapped. Then you follow through with the Level One directions. The ghost's name is written on a piece of paper and stuffed in a bottle with the hotfoot powder. Cork the top and throw into Bone River.'

Claire stood on her knees beside Henry. "We have enough small bags of the pine needles and sage for each of us."

"Good. Make sure we have all the materials, Claire. Go ahead and place the bowl in your backpack. We can each carry a bag of the needles and sage. I will pack the box of stones in my backpack."

Claire went into action. Henry helped. They packed each backpack with all the necessary ingredients. They reviewed and made sure everyone had supplies for Level One and Level Two ghosts.

"Grab another bag of the hotfoot powder, Henry. Half the bag from last time has been used," Claire said.

While Claire and Henry packed, Wendy read. Flipping through the pages, she surprisingly found a picture of the same pocket watch Mrs. Harper owned. "This was not here the last time I looked in the journal," Wendy murmured. "It couldn't have been." She breezed over the page looking back at the top under the title. The page had been written by…Caroline Jean Harper?

Chapter Twenty-five

In Mrs. Harper's own handwriting, Wendy began to read what was written on the page about the mysterious watch.

'If you are reading this, then the watch has been activated, the spells have begun, and I have been kidnapped.'

Wendy's mouth flew open.

'I was sworn to secrecy by the first owners of the store. They were sworn by Mrs. Lorna Grapples. No one knows the secrets of this pocket watch or the powers it holds now, but me. For protection, my sister, Mimi Elsie Taylor, does not know of the special powers it possesses. It is best. For Mrs. Lorna Grapples was a witch. And in the wrong hands, Bridgeville could change forever.'

Wendy's eyes went wide. She looked up at Claire and Henry. They were too busy stuffing the backpacks to notice her surprised look. She looked back at the pages and continued reading.

'After Abner Grapples humiliated his wife at his birthday party, Lorna knew Abner would never change. The next day she took the watch and had it engraved with a unique incantation on the inside of the lid. She then placed an old and very ancient spell on the watch. In order to make the spell work a person, who is alive, must read the incantation. Lorna Grapples paid the owners well to keep the watch, and the secret. For the watch can bring the deceased back to life.'

Chills ran down Wendy's spine. "Claire and Henry, are you finished?"

"We are now," Claire said, zipping up the final backpack.

Henry looked over at Wendy and saw how pale she was. "What's wrong, Wendy?"

Wendy didn't know any other way to tell them, so she started talking. She told them all about the watch. From the day Lefty Lennie screamed for it, to when Mrs. Taylor told the story about it at the library, to today when her dad handed her the watch, and the majority of what she had just read in Finger Bones' leather journal.

"I knew when Dad handed me the pocket watch it was the one Lefty Lennie wanted, but I didn't understand why. Now I do. Let me read this part." Wendy paused and looked at Claire and Henry. "By the way, Mrs. Harper wrote this entire page on the watch." Without giving them time to respond, she found her spot in the journal, and started reading.

'Mimi Elsie Taylor does not know of the special powers it possesses. It is best. For Mrs. Lorna Grapples was a witch. And in the wrong hands, Bridgeville could change forever.'"

Claire made a loud gasp and grabbed Henry by the arm.

"Hey, you're getting mean with those fingernails today," Henry yelled. "They are digging holes in my arm."

Claire did not let go.

"Mrs. Harper has it all written down here in the book about how Mrs. Lorna put a spell on the watch," Wendy said.

"From everything we know so far and all I have read here, I believe Lefty Lennie is here to get the watch for whoever The Boss is. The Boss will then use the watch to return to the living."

Claire looked scared. "Are we talking the Wicked Witch of the West or the Good Witch of the North?"

"Duh," Henry answered. "Mrs. Lorna had to be a good witch."

Wendy shook her head. "I thought Abner Grapples might be The Boss. But he was never told about the spell on the watch. Mrs. Lorna paid the first owners a lot of money for the watch, paid a lot to have it engraved, and paid them a large amount to keep it a secret. And I know Mrs. Harper had no reason to tell anyone?"

"Lefty Lennie worked for Abner Grapples. He may have found out some way," Henry suggested. He raised both his hands and wiggled his fingers. "He may have done some Hocus Pocus on the watch too."

"He may have, Henry," Wendy said, thinking about it.

"Lorna Grapples was a witch, huh?" Henry asked.

"I guess so. Says it right here in Finger Bones' journal," Wendy answered. "She must have been a good witch. She never hurt her husband when he was alive. And look at what all he had had done to her."

Claire became more upset. "I just thought about something. The ghosts have Mrs. Harper, and she has no idea where the watch is since Mrs. Taylor took it to get fixed."

"I know," Wendy said.

"What will they do to her?" Claire asked in a trembling voice.

"Well if all of this is true, those ghosts aren't going to take a chance. They will not hurt Mrs. Harper. They need her alive to find the watch," Wendy said.

"And they need her alive to read the incantation on the watch," Henry said.

"You're right," Wendy said. "Oh, one more thing I thought about. While Dad was on the phone with Mrs. Taylor, she told him I would know what to do with the watch."

"Really?" Claire asked. She began to relax and think. "Hum, Mrs. Harper wrote in Finger Bones' journal. Mrs. Taylor didn't know what the watch would do, but she did read the writing on the inside of the lid where it pops open. So, she at least knew about that."

"Yes she did," Wendy said. "Good thinking. And she probably knows, by now, the watch has some kind of powers…"

"I think the sisters are witches too," Henry interrupted with his eyebrows raised. He reached down and tied one his shoelaces. "You know what else?"

"What?" Wendy said, holding the journal close to her chest.

"We all knew the sisters were very fond of Finger Bones."

Then it hit Wendy. Excited, she pointed at Henry and began to talk as fast as she could before he could say another word. "And you think they knew about Finger Bones and his job. And now they know it's my job. And Mrs. Harper knew I would look in the journal. You think somehow she managed to place the information about the pocket watch in the leather journal, so I would see it."

Henry looked baffled. "Well, no. I just meant they were fond of Finger Bones."

"I think you're right, Wendy," Claire said, sounding more chipper. "This is a lot of information to process. Okay, we know that the ghosts have Mrs. Harper. We now know they want this pocket watch, and we think they want the pocket watch because it brings the dead back to life."

"Don't forget the sisters are probably witches too," Henry said, waving his arms to get their attention.

Claire suddenly unzipped her backpack and shuffled some of the items around. Henry's arm waving in the air didn't seem to be working.

"Um, Wendy, we made need more than Level Two items," Claire said looking grim. Look further on through the book and see what else you kind find. We may be dealing with another ghost, a meaner and cleverer ghost."

Wendy looked back down at the journal. "I think so, Claire. Let me see," Wendy said, flipping over two pages.

She began reading out loud.

" 'Level Three ghosts can choose to be transparent or solid. They can transform into any human form. They can choose to be fuzzy or clear. They are hideous looking when the evil side takes over.

When Level Three ghosts travel from place to place, good ghosts may have a white fog around them. The evil ghosts travel with a dark black cloud or black smoke. They suck the energy from other ghosts making them stronger. A Level Three ghosts can also transform into a fog or mist at any time they choose, especially when they need to escape.' "

Wendy flipped the page. The title read *Sending Level Three Ghosts to Their Next Destination.* In the middle of the page was a drawing of the Graveyard Dirt. Wendy gazed over the drawing. Graveyard Dirt was not to be handled lightly. But she knew this was the only way to handle the ghost once and for all. She had to use the Graveyard Dirt of Lefty Lennie Spinsters.

Wendy read fast.

"Level Three ghosts are difficult to send to their next destination. But it can be accomplished. Be prepared and ready to move fast. Follow the guidelines of the Level Two ghosts. While the ghost is trapped by the obsidian stones take the Graveyard Dirt and sprinkle the entire bag over a white plate. Then leave the bag on top of the dirt. Place any type of iron piece into the bag.

It's best to use a six inch piece of iron. With the dirt and iron piece on top, wrap the plate in a red cloth or red handkerchief, tying it with a string. Bury it over the ghost's grave. For best results, take two or three people to help. One can bury the Graveyard Dirt while the other two take care of the bottle, throwing it in Bone River. When all of the above has been accomplished, the ghost will be sent to their next place of business. Evil ghosts will blow up.'"

287

Wendy stopped and looked up at Claire.

Henry started waving again. "If you two would pay attention to me for one second, you both would see I have everything ready. Everything Wendy read about capturing and sending Level Two and now Level Three ghosts. I have it all right here."

Wendy and Claire turned their heads at the same time toward Henry.

Henry pointed at the three backpacks. "I have the Graveyard dirt in the front compartment of your backpack, Wendy. It's sitting upright. See," he said, patting the outside of the pocket on the backpack. "It's a snug fit. It will not budge." He unzipped the large area of the backpack. "You had an old white plate on the shelf. It's here." He lifted the plate showing Wendy. "And I put the old string and red handkerchief I had in my pack and placed it here beside the plate. See the string. I tied it loosely around the end of the handkerchief so you can easily find it." Henry zipped the compartment and made sure all other backpacks were zipped and ready to go.

"I have one more thing I want to take." Wendy stood and walked over to where one of the horseshoes was hanging. She removed a piece of string. "Claire, tie this on me please. This is the string Finger Bones gave me the night he died. Remember, I had it in my hand."

"I remember," she said softly, tying the string on Wendy's wrist. "Okay, it's tied."

"Then everything is ready. Let's go catch us some ghosts," Henry said.

Chapter Twenty-six

Wendy, along with Claire and Henry, slung their backpacks over their shoulders and jumped on their bikes. They didn't slow their pace when they reached Screaming Hollow Road. Wendy glanced at Finger Bones' destroyed home. The wreckage made her more determined to succeed in capturing Lefty Lennie and The Boss. Soon they reached the path leading to the old cemetery which was located at the top of the hill.

"We'll leave the bikes here. Follow me," Wendy said in a low voice.

Adjusting their backpacks, they began hiking up the hill toward the cemetery. Halfway up the hill, Wendy stopped. Claire and Henry halted beside her. The three gazed up the dark trail. The darkness looked like a door which led to another world.

They made their way through the thick woods. Upon nearing the grave sites, Wendy looked on both sides of the path at the overgrown shrubbery Mrs. Harper had spoken of. Scattered sage and catnip flourished throughout the brush. The three crept along looking up and gawking at the branches, hanging low on the trees. The branches dipped down and looked like claws, reaching and waiting for their chance to grab an intruder.

The abandoned cemetery hid inside a rusted iron fence on a large hill with overgrown bushes, covering the outside. Many of the headstones and statues were still standing inside the burial ground. All were covered in some type of moss or fungus. Some of the graves had cracked. The narrow path led straight to the gate of the forbidden looking site.

Wendy held up her hand for Claire and Henry to stop. "Listen. I hear voices."

All three cocked their heads. Voices were heard coming from inside the cemetery. Wendy swiftly tiptoed towards the fence. She grabbed her nose as soon as the awful odor she had endured before hit her nostrils. The stench quickly hit Claire and Henry's noses as the three squatted between the thick rows of bushes behind the rustic iron fence.

"But Boss, I tried. She's not changing her story. She says she doesn't have the pocket watch. I even tied the old battle ax to a chair and put the bright lights on her all day."

"Hush you bumbling idiot. What's happened to you? You use to scare the strongest and meanest humans. Now kids and an old woman are getting the best of you."

Wendy eyebrows came together. She didn't recognize this voice scolding so harshly. It was a high pitched, raspy voice, a female voice. A closer look and Wendy saw the croaky voice was talking to Lefty Lennie. Wendy carefully pushed back a branch and peered through the fence. Claire and Henry leaned in also to see if they could catch part of the conversation.

Sinking deeper and deeper into the bush, Wendy's eyes went wider with surprise, for right in the line of her vision stood the ghost of…Mrs. Lorna Grapples. Seeing Mrs. Grapples startled Wendy so much, she flew backwards. Claire and Henry jumped up and saved Wendy just in the nick of time before she hit the ground.

Wendy recognized Mrs. Grapples by the newspaper clippings. She looked very different as a ghost than what she remembered from the pictures. This Mrs. Grapples had become disfigured. Her pearl-white skin had become bumpy and rough. Wendy saw Mrs. Grapples facing Lefty Lennie. Her eyes glared angrily at him. The white glow that always cascaded off Finger Bones did not flow from her. Dusty black smut flew from her. The hate her husband had carried in life seemed to dwell in the horrible ghost standing in front of Wendy now.

The bushes jiggled and shook. Wendy, Claire, and Henry remained in their positions on the ground hoping Lefty

Lennie and Mrs. Grapples hadn't heard their movements. Claire had Wendy under one arm and Henry had her under the other. Wendy felt Claire shaking, and Henry wasn't much better. Beads of sweat had popped out on his temples.

Wendy scooted her feet back to gain her balance. "The ghost talking to Lefty Lennie is Mrs. Grapples," Wendy whispered.

"What? It's not mean old Mr. Grapples?" Claire asked shocked.

Wendy shook her head. "Go look for yourself."

Claire and Henry eased up to the fence.

Wendy leaned to her right and crawled over to the gate. She peered through the iron rods and gawked at the two ghosts, standing inside the burial grounds.

Lefty Lennie Spinsters stood before Mrs. Lorna Grapples gritting his teeth. Wendy saw Mrs. Grapples' face twisted in a rage.

"We are running out of time," Mrs. Grapples snapped. She swirled away from Lefty Lennie and jerked her head back. "Look at the moon. The full moon will occur in less than one hour. I must have that pocket watch before it's at its peak in order to bring my husband back to life."

Wendy watched in horror as the witch raised her fists in the air.

"Where are those meddling kids when you *do* want them? I need the little human girl, the one chosen by the stick. She has to be the one who reads the incantation as the moon is reaching its fullness."

Wendy heard Henry sneeze. She knew it was him. When he sneezed it sounded like an old man, snorting loudly. Wendy hit the ground on her stomach and threw her arms over her head. "No, no, no, Henry."

Wendy lay perfectly still. She heard the swooshing of leaves. Twigs crunched. Then a loud stomping noise was heard coming out of the brush.

"Claire, Henry, don't be so loud. Do you want to get us caught? Henry, they could've heard you," Wendy said, sitting up and brushing the dirt and leaves from her pants.

The stomping stopped.

Wendy looked down at the ground in front of her. She saw three sets of shoes. She recognized the pair of shoes on the left, and the ones on the right. As she looked up, Wendy discovered Lefty Lennie wore the ones in the middle and he had a tight grip of the backpacks strapped to Claire and Henry's shoulders.

"Sorry, Wendy," Henry said, whining. "I'm allergic to the bushes."

"Don't worry about it, Henry," Wendy said. She looked up at Lefty Lennie and stared him straight in his bloodshot eyes. Situating the backpack on her shoulders, she said, "Take me to your leader."

Lefty Lennie growled and pushed Claire and Henry forward. They stumbled several steps toward the gate. Wendy turned and unlatched it. The three friends entered the isolated cemetery walking side by side.

Wendy could hear the overgrown ghost, stomping behind her. Her brain began to think. She stopped and reached into her pocket.

"What are you doing?" Lefty growled from behind her.

"It's called bubblegum," Wendy said, holding up the gum for him to see and then plopping it in her mouth. I had to throw away the other gum. It didn't have any more taste. She dropped her arm by her side and allowed the wrapper to fall freely to the damp grass.

"All three of you, start walking!" Lefty Lennie roared.

Startled by his command, the three jumped and began to walk. Wendy had no idea where they were going as they moved through the creepy grounds with Lefty Lennie at their heels.

Wendy gazed around at the large trees, shrubbery, and plants that grew within the iron fence of the large cemetery. All of it gave off a mystical feel as they weaved around the eerie old tombstones. She led the way to wherever they were going by the well-lit moon. Every few seconds, she heard Claire make a gasping sound. The light from the moon cast shadows over the tombstones causing spooky images to jump and dance. Wendy imagined Henry's legs were dancing more than the shadows.

Wendy chewed her gum silently. It helped her to think and helped to keep her calm. As she walked, she decided to ask Lefty Lennie a few questions to see if she could get any kind of information out of him. He couldn't do anything to her yet. She now knew the witch needed her for the spell to work. "Where did Mrs. Grapples go, Lefty?"

"That's none of your concern."

"Is Lorna Grapple your boss now?"

"What if she is?" he snarled.

"Why are you working for her? I thought you worked for Mr. Grapples."

"I work for her until the Full Moon. He will be in power then."

"Who will be in power?" Wendy asked, stopping and turning to face Lefty. Claire and Henry stepped to the side so Wendy could see Lefty. They knew when she chewed gum it was best to stay quiet, watch, and listen.

"That's enough talk." A voice from behind Wendy ordered.

Wendy whirled around.

There stood before them the ugly Mrs. Grapples with her head held high like a queen. "Come stand with me, Lennie." She grinned wickedly. "I have something to show the sweet children."

Lefty transformed back into his ghost form and floated to her side.

Mrs. Lorna then slowly moved to one side. There sitting in a chair tied with a rope and gagged was Mrs. Harper.

Chapter Twenty-seven

"Mrs. Harper, are you all right?" the children hollered.

She tried to answer, but only mumbled words emerged.

"What have you done to her? Her head is bleeding,"
Wendy shouted, narrowing her brows. She made a step
forward.

"Stop right where you are little girl. No one touches a
hair on her until we have resurrected my husband. Do I make
myself clear?" Mrs. Lorna's eyes grew dark.

Black smut emerged from her body. It reminded
Wendy of the energy Lefty Lennie sucked down his throat
from the poor ghost at the jail.

Lefty Lennie cackled.

"I'll read the incantation if you let me untie her,"
Wendy said angrily.

The ugly hag glanced at the moon. Her features turned uglier. Scabs formed on her wrinkled skin and her fingernails began to curl and sharpen. She lurched in front of Wendy and was so close their noses almost touched. "My dear girl, there will be no compromises until you do as I say. And if you do not cooperate, there will be consequences I doubt you can live with," she hissed. She then whirled and glided over to two nearby graves.

Looking at the headstones, Wendy read the names. Engraved on one headstone was Mr. Abner Grapples and on the other was Mrs. Lorna Grapples

At that moment, the ugly witch pointed her crooked and warty finger toward her husband's grave and began chanting odd words. Wendy noticed the concrete slab had started to quiver and shake. The tall headstone shook. Slowly, the grave opened.

Wendy's head became dizzy. She looked down and blinked several times trying to focus. She felt sick. Claire and

Henry eased up beside her. They had become queasy too. Bent over with nausea, all three could hear the most horrible sound, slithering and oozing its way closer to the opening of the grave.

Wendy looked up and over at Mrs. Harper.

Mrs. Harper gave Wendy a tiny, encouraging smile. *Wendy, fight the sickness. It's nothing but an illusion. It's a trick. You are here to do something good. Believe in yourself.*

Wendy stood goggling at Mrs. Harper. *Is this real? Am I really hearing you?*

Isn't magic fun? Mrs. Harper continued to look at Wendy, but her mouth did not move. *Read the incantation, Wendy. Then finish the job.* She looked over and glared at the two ghosts. *And please hurry! These two floaters are grating on my nerves.*

Wendy stood a moment more. She then took a deep breath and let out a low sigh. Turning to the two chanting spirits, she said, "Okay, I'll do it."

Claire and Henry jerked their heads toward Wendy in disbelief. Their eyes were large.

"It will be okay, trust me." Wendy said, and hoped. Opening the backpack, she removed the box the watch was in, and then looked back up at Claire and Henry.

They were still gawking at her.

"Please, just do what I say without any questions." Wendy pulled the top off the box and removed the watch. Slowly, she opened the lid. "Claire, I need for you to write the name Abner Grapples on a piece of the paper."

Claire shook her head sideways quickly. She then hurried over and knelt beside Wendy. Henry stood behind Claire watching.

The ugly hag stopped laughing. Her eyes grew large when she saw the gold piece. She held up a fist in victory. She yelled, "Finally, now my love, we will be together forever. And you shall rule the town of Bridgeville with me at your side!"

Wendy heard the ugly hag and her purpose. Then Mrs. Harper spoke again. Wendy heard her uplifting words. *Wendy, the Winds of Time will only work when it knows you are working for the good. You are good.*

"What are you waiting for, girl? Read it now." the ugly hag demanded. "The moon is reaching its fullness."

Lefty Lennie flexed his muscles and his eyes turned dark. "Do what she says," he rumbled. He stomped his heavy foot and shook his fist.

With her hands shaking, Claire handed Wendy the horribly scribbled name on the paper. Wendy crammed the paper into the compartment and then shut the lids. The ticking grew louder. The sound of it beat like the rhythm of a heartbeat.

Wendy then heard the unnerving crawling in the grave. A slurping and gurgling sound emerged from the ground.

"Come my darling," the ugly hag said sweetly. The slurping sound abruptly stopped. The old hag screeched. She swirled to face Wendy. "Read it now!" The ugly hag whirled over to and hovered over Mrs. Harper. "Read or she will die!" she screamed.

Wendy stood where the light of the moon bounced off the watch. She began to read in earnest. *"'The Winds of Time I call to unlock, the passage which has been blocked.'"*

Wendy paused. With wide eyes she looked above the burial ground where Abner Grapples now lay. Dark clouds, which had been scattered in the night skies, gathered and loomed overhead. Claws of lightning lit up the clouds. The moon glowed brighter. It looked bigger and larger with each passing second.

Wendy looked back at the watch and continued to read. *"'A name and place enclosed you will find, bring past to present I plead you to bind.'"*

At the moment she finished the incantation a strong wind scooped the watch from Wendy's grasp. It disappeared into the night skies.

The old hags decaying outfit violently flapped in the wind. Most of her hair had fallen from the carefully placed bobby pins. Her hair was flipping in the wind wildly. While Wendy read the incantation, the old hag had made her way back over to her husband's grave. She and Lefty Lennie watched with eager eyes as something from below started to emerge.

Chapter Twenty-eight

Wendy and her friends were forgotten as the two ghosts waited for The Boss to appear.

The three took the opportunity and ran to Mrs. Harper. Henry tried desperately to untie the knotted ropes.

"Henry, hurry!" Claire shouted over the noise of the wind and thunder.

Wendy glanced over at the old hag hovering over the grave. The witch looked darker and even more evil. "Henry, do something."

"I can't loosen the knot," he shouted. He swung his backpack to the ground and grabbed a knife from his backpack. He cut the ropes from her hands and feet, and then released her. They helped her up and all four ran and hid behind an enormous headstone.

Wendy peeped from one corner of the tomb. Claire and Henry looked from the other end. From the grim grave, they watched a ghastly hand. The fingers were grasping and digging at the fresh soil. Bugs ran from the opening and worms squirmed from the loose dirt. The spell had begun. The Winds of Time were definitely at work.

Mrs. Harper did not seem concerned. She sat resting with her back against the tombstone. "I should think the spell will begin backfiring in a few seconds," Mrs. Harper said loudly. "And when it does Wendy, you three continue with the plan."

Wendy glanced back at Mrs. Harper. *What?* Above the clouds began to twirl and loop over the old hag and Lefty Lennie. Then one streak of lightning suddenly bolted down hitting Abner's decaying hand. He bellowed with pain and rage. Wendy then understood. "Claire, Henry, let's get everything ready. We're going to send Lefty Lennie on his way."

"The Winds of Time will take care of Abner and Lorna Grapples," Mrs. Harper yelled above the increasing noise. "I took care of that when I cast the spell and wrote in Finger Bones' journal. Glad to see it worked," she said, clasping her hands together pleased.

Wendy shook her finger at Mrs. Harper. "You are the smartest and most wonderful lady, Mrs. Harper!"

"Well, I think you are too, Wendy," she said, looking at Wendy. "Now, let's go and get us a ghost. I've been waiting for a chance such as this for a long time."

Wendy smiled. "Then I know just what you can do."

***

The ugly hag looked down. "No! This can't be happening!" she screamed, looking down at the grave. She howled above the storm at Lefty Lennie. "Do something you overgrown toad. Help my husband."

Lefty Lennie bent his knees, leaned over, and grabbed the disgusting hand which had emerged from the old grave. He pulled with all his might. But instead of pulling out The Boss, Lefty Lennie snapped and broke off the hand from the wrist when he yanked. It wiggled in his hands and then burst into flames. Lefty Lennie extended his arm, dropped the hand, and jumped back.

The ugly hag looked down at her hands and her feet. She screamed. Her body turned a gooey dark translucent. She bellowed in agony and then burst into a black powder. The energy she had taken from other ghosts had taken over her.

***

Barricaded behind the huge headstone, Claire and Henry hurriedly prepared the bottle. Wendy removed the obsidian stones. She grabbed three of them, and Mrs. Harper picked up the other two. Cautiously, they worked their way toward Lefty Lennie.

While he stood in shock, Wendy and Mrs. Harper set out the obsidian stones. At the moment the last one was placed an electrical cage appeared and trapped the ghost.

Lefty Lennie threw his head back and roared. He stomped and beat the cage.

"Good job, Wendy!" Mrs. Harper exclaimed, giving Wendy a high five.

"We make a pretty good team, don't we?" Wendy yelled back.

"We sure do young lady." Mrs. Harper looked and spotted the pile of ashes. "Looks like Mrs. Lorna will not be bothering anyone anymore. She found out the hard way what happens when you mess with The Winds of Time."

Looking to see, Wendy saw the pile. She also saw another ghost standing over the remains of the hag. It was an old man sprinkling a sparkling white powder over the pile, which was turning it white. He was holding a mason jar that seemed to contain the magic. "Who's he and what's he doing?" Wendy hollered.

"That's Sam Ballard. Don't worry. He's the Events Director. He's making sure the powder will not be blown away by the winds. It freezes and causes anything it's sprinkled on to stick."

"Ah, so he's Sam Ballard. He looks a lot like Finger Bones. I was told about him the day the stick chose me." Wendy looked back at Mrs. Harper. "Now for the part you've been waiting for, Mrs. Harper." They hurried back to the tombstone.

"We have the bottle ready, Wendy," Henry hollered.

The clouds overhead twirled faster. The lightning strikes forked out more and the trees and their branches leaned further.

"Hurry to the river," Wendy shouted. "Mrs. Harper and I will take care of the rest. We have Lefty Lennie caged."

Claire and Henry jumped up to see. Sparks of fire flew as Lefty Lennie slammed his fists into the electrical cage. When he saw them staring, his bellow shook the ground.

"Claire, Henry, hurry to Bone River," Mrs. Harper shouted. "And be careful. The lady who controls the Winds of Time will be unhappy until we can send this final ghost to its next place. Until then, she will continue to show her fury."

"Wait, Claire, I need the bowl and the matches from your backpack," Wendy yelled.

Claire nodded her head, quickly found the items, and tossed them to Wendy. Claire then took off running behind Henry to the gate.

Wendy quickly poured the small bags of sage and pine needles into the bowl. She grabbed the matches. Holding her hand over the top the bowl, Wendy ran to where Lefty Lennie stood trapped. Amazingly, the wind stood still where she crouched to light the match.

"Whoever is helping me, thank you," she said, lighting the sage and pine needles.

"You're welcome," a deep and familiar voice replied.

Wendy looked up and there was Finger Bones. He was shining and glowing. He stood holding the stick with the bindle over the bowl. A transparent dome began to form over Wendy and the bowl. "Go ahead and light it. This will hold the wind off long enough for you to get rid of this cantankerous ghost."

"Wow! Thanks a bunch."

"You're welcome."

Wendy jogged back to the tombstone. On her knees and facing Mrs. Harper, she took out the white plate and red handkerchief from her backpack. She removed the string from the end of the handkerchief and placed it between her teeth. Mrs. Harper then grabbed the handkerchief and spread it the best she could on the ground up next to the tombstone. It was a struggle. The winds blew hard as Wendy placed the plate in the middle. She then removed the bag labeled, Graveyard Dirt. She and Mrs. Harper tried to shield the plate from the wind.

"Would you like a little help?" Finger Bones hollered. He held the stick and again magically formed a protective dome.

"Well hey, old friend," Mrs. Harper hollered over the wind. "I didn't see you pop in."

"How's the cut on your head?"

"It's fine. We've been in worse shape, haven't we?"

"Yes we have, Mrs. Harper. We sure have."

Wendy carefully poured the dirt from Lefty Lennie's grave onto the plate and laid the empty bag on top of it.

She then looked at Mrs. Harper in horror. "Oh no, I forgot the iron to place in the bag."

Mrs. Harper looked around. "Wait right here." She hurried to a nearby grave where there was a broken wrought iron fence. Mrs. Harper returned with a piece almost ten inches long. "I thought a longer piece would do the trick," she said.

The two worked together and wrapped the plate. They then tied the string to the end of the red handkerchief. It was ready.

Finger Bones put the bindle down. "Good job, ladies." He then disappeared.

"Let's get this over to Lefty Lennie's grave, bury this potion, and take care of this trouble making ghost," Mrs. Harper said.

Wendy held the plate as Mrs. Harper guided her around several graves to the gravesite. Surprisingly, a shovel was conveniently propped against the headstone. Wendy looked at Mrs. Harper. Together they said, "Finger Bones."

"Wendy went to work digging. The soil was loose, so it didn't take long before she was able to place the red handkerchief containing the items inside the hole. She reached down to make sure the string was tied tight around it. She then quickly covered the hole and patted the dirt on top.

"We are finished with our part," Wendy hollered. "I Know Claire and Henry will have their part complete soon too."

"I have no doubt," she said loudly. She tapped Wendy on the shoulder and pointed to a small shed. "Must be where they kept some of the groundkeeper's equipment. Come on."

They luckily found the shed unlocked and hurried inside, closing and securing the door behind them. Wendy looked around and found an old coat. She removed it from the hook, shook it, and gave it to Mrs. Harper to wear. Wendy then sat beside her. They sat quietly and listened to the wind slam against the shed.

"I know Mrs. Taylor is worried about you," Wendy said.

"Well, by this time, I'm sure your father is worried about you."

Wendy sat listening to the storm. "Mrs. Taylor, the watch, it flew out of my hands after I read the incantation."

"It's okay dear. I know. The lady who controls the Winds of Time took the watch. She will destroy it to guarantee this will never happen again." Mrs. Harper cupped her hand to her ear. "Oh listen. The wind has stopped."

Everything had turned peaceful outside the shed. The wind calmed to a gentle breeze and the lightning stopped popping in the sky. Wendy and Mrs. Harper unlatched the door to the shed, peeked outside, and slowly stepped onto the wet grass.

Wendy looked all around at the scattered leaves and branches. They covered the ground and the headstones. She then gazed up at the night sky. The clouds were slowly scattering and they were leaving behind a clear sky and stars. The Full Moon glowed.

Wendy and Mrs. Harper walked back to Abner and Lorna Grapples' graves. Lefty Lennie was gone. There was nothing left, but a large burnt spot and a pile of ashes. Wendy walked over to the dark pile of black powder where Mrs. Grapples had stood.

Wendy glanced over at Mrs. Harper. She had two jars in her hands. "I always come prepared. Here, you scoop up all you can of her. I'll get Lennie. I have one more mason jar in my pocket for old man Grapples' ashes from his hand. Never know when we might need these."

When finished, they collected the stones and headed for the gate of the cemetery. Soon they heard someone hollering and calling their names. They stopped briefly to listen. "Wendy, are you here? Mrs. Harper, it is Captain Winkelmann."

Wendy smiled and yelled. "Over here, Dad! We're over here!"

Mr. Winkelmann appeared over a hill. "There you two are," he said. Wendy could tell her dad was proud to see her. She was definitely proud to see him. "I have Claire and Henry waiting in the car. I found them down the dirt road. Your Mom is over at the Rubottom Plantation sitting with Mrs. Taylor. Mrs. Harper, are you okay?"

"Why, I am fine, Captain Winkelmann. I couldn't be in better hands," she said, wrapping an arm around Wendy.

"Dad, Mrs. Harper has a nasty cut on her head."

Mr. Winkelmann walked up to Mrs. Harper and pushed some of her hair back. "Yep, I think Henry was correct. Someone is going to need a few stitches." After checking to make sure Mrs. Harper was okay, Mr. Winkelmann gave Wendy a big hug.

"Dad, how did you find us in this big cemetery?"

"I saw the bubblegum wrapper you left behind. It was stuck on the gate. And when Claire and Henry left you two to go and get help, Henry had taken one of his TV guides and had torn it into pieces making a trail. The giblets of paper lead me straight to you. He said he knew his TV guides were worth something." He lifted his cap and scratched his head. "What I can't figure out is why the paper didn't blow away in all the wind we had earlier."

Wendy didn't respond. Her night had been filled with weird happenings.

Mr. Winkelmann fixed his cap and then looked down at his daughter. "Wendy, you gave us a scare young lady."

"Please don't be mad at her, Odus. It was my fault for coming up here alone. Wendy remembered I visited my husband's grave and she came looking for me," Mrs. Taylor bragged, giving Wendy a small hug.

Mr. Winkelmann looked at his daughter and ruffled her hair. "I can't be too mad then. I'm proud of you, Wendy."

"To show my gratitude, and since it is a Friday night, please let Wendy and her friends spend the night with my sister and me. The girls can sleep in the guest room and there is a comfortable couch in the downstairs den. It can be let out into a bed for Henry."

Mr. Winkelmann glanced at Wendy.

Wendy gave her dad a pleading look.

"Oh, all right," he told Wendy. "If your mother says it is okay, then it's okay with me. I'll get her to call Claire and Henry's parents." He looked at Mrs. Harper. "But first, you're going straight to the emergency room to see Dr. Cooper. I think you're going to need some stitches."

Chapter Twenty-nine

"Hey, don't hog all the popcorn," Claire yelled at Henry.

"Nope, I'm not sharing this bowl. Mrs. Taylor said I could eat the entire bowl and that's just what I plan to do."

"I don't see where you're putting it after eating five pieces of barbequed chicken, a plate full of mashed potatoes, and four of Mrs. Taylor's homemade yeast rolls."

"What can I say, I'm a growing boy."

"Here we go," Mrs. Taylor said, appearing with two more huge bowls of buttery popcorn.

Mrs. Harper scooted up in her comfortable chair. "Let me help you with that sister."

"Oh no, you sit right where you are and relax. The doctor said you should take it easy. It took five stitches you know. Plus, I am the hostess tonight." She passed one bowl over for Wendy and Claire to share. Mrs. Harper and she shared the other.

After they all got cozy, Wendy listened to everyone explain their own version of the night's events. Wendy, Claire, and Henry were correct in guessing the sisters were witches. And Mrs. Taylor, she understood why her sister had kept the true secret of the pocket watch, and was not upset one bit. Though, she was a little troubled with herself. If she had not had the watch fixed, she wouldn't have started the spell.

Mrs. Harper told about how Lefty Lennie acted at the cemetery and what he looked like when he was scared. Mrs. Taylor laughed. Wendy smiled seeing the two sisters together, laughing and enjoying each other's company. To see Claire's face while the stories were being told was priceless. Her fearless friend grabbed Henry every time someone told a part about the ugly hag or about old man Grapples crawling from the grave. Henry was jumpy too.

While facing the ghosts tonight, Wendy admitted to herself it was frightening. Although, she also had to admit, ghost hunting was exciting too. She finally felt she was doing something important. She was protecting Bridgeville, and her friends were helping her.

While they all sat giggling and laughing, Finger Bones had popped in. He sat in a chair next to the fireplace. Wendy saw him first. She jolted up and said, "Finger Bones, glad you could come."

Everyone stopped talking and looked.

"I received your invitation by Mrs. Taylor. I heard the good news. Well done on your first job."

"Thanks, Finger Bones. But I didn't do it. We all did. Even Mrs. Harper helped send Lefty Lennie Spinsters to his next destination."

"And the Winds of Time took care of Mrs. Grapples and old man Grapples." Claire said.

Wendy turned her head sideways. "What happened to you tonight? You disappeared."

Finger Bones propped the stick against his knee. When he looked back up he changed his expression. He smiled. Wendy couldn't tell if he was looking at her or something behind her.

"Oh, I went to check on someone else we all know. He decided he would come with me. He wants to tell the new team of ghost hunters something."

"What?" the three friends asked.

"I want to say too, great job tonight," said a familiar voice behind Wendy. "I heard you guys were all right!"

Wendy whirled around. Willie Porter stood happily, rocking back and forth on his heels.

"Hey, Willie," Henry shouted. "Man, am I glad to see you. I thought you were a goner."

"You can thank the lady who controls the Winds of Time."

"Have you seen her?" Henry asked.

"Yep, I sure have. She's nice too."

A large fog appeared beside Willie. The fog turned into a fuzzy figure, and then into Sam.

"Wendy, Claire, and Henry, officially meet Sam Ballard," Finger Bones said proudly.

All three friends turned and said hello.

"It's so nice to meet each of you, the youngest floater hunters we've ever had. I wanted to tell you myself what a great job all of you did tonight."

"Thank you for helping me tonight, Mr. Sam," Wendy said.

"You're very welcome young lady. As the Events Director, I try to help in any way I can."

"Sam and I have been friends for a very long time," Finger Bones said.

Sam gave a chuckle.

Mrs. Harper held up her glass of tea. "Well, now that we're all here, I say we need to make a toast to the good work *we all* did tonight."

Everyone stood.

"I would like to say how proud I am of Wendy, Claire, and Henry," Mrs. Taylor announced. "You each have shown such bravery tonight. Even when you were thrown terrible obstacles, you stuck together and succeeded. And Wendy, my dear little one, thanks for staying with Sister and bringing her home to me." Mrs. Taylor had tears in her eyes. "You *all* are my heroes."

Wendy, Claire, and Henry toasted their tea glasses with Mrs. Taylor and Mrs. Harper.

Finger Bones smiled. "See, I told you, Wendy. Everything will be fine. Everything is as it should be."

Finger Bones gazed around at everyone. He took in a deep breath and let out a sigh.

Wendy saw his mood change and walked over to stand beside his chair. "Okay Finger Bones, what's going on?" she asked in a low voice. "Something is bothering you. I can see it in your eyes."

"Let's walk to the front porch. No need in worrying everyone. They're having such a good time."

Wendy followed Finger Bones to the porch. Both stood outside looking up at the night sky. "The moon is still showing bright and beautiful tonight," he said.

Wendy gazed up at the moon. It was hard for her to believe earlier tonight this same moon was used for such an evil act. The spell and incantation almost worked. Then it hit Wendy. She knew what was bothering Finger Bones. "I know what you're worried about. It's Abner Grapples. You know he will try to figure another way to come back."

"You're very smart to be ten years old."

"I will be eleven soon."

Finger Bones looked at her and gave a tiny smile. "You really did a good job tonight, Wendy."

"I can do this. You think I'm too young, but I'm not. The stick chose me. You said yourself it wouldn't have chosen me if it didn't think I could handle it."

"That's true." He gazed back up at the moon. "So, you're willing to accept that Abner Grapples is out there somewhere? And when he tries to resurface..."

"I'll be prepared, Finger Bones."

"Well, okay then. That's good enough for me," he said satisfied. He turned and looked inside the window. Everyone was enjoying each other's company. "Tonight is a celebration.

I think the whereabouts and the plans of Abner Grapples can

wait until tomorrow then."

Yes, Wendy thought. *That would have to be another*

story.

Made in the USA
Charleston, SC
27 October 2012